VEN. POMNYUN SUNIM
A TASTE OF ENLIGHTENMENT

A TASTE OF ENLIGHTENMENT
Stories from Seon Buddhism

©VEN. POMNYUN SUNIM, 2022

First Edition	October 20, 2022
Published by	Jungto Publishing
	42 Hyoryeong-ro 51-gil, Seocho-gu, Seoul, Korea
	tel. +82-2-587-8991
	e-mail. jungtobook@gmail.com
Written by	Ven. Pomnyun Sunim
Translated by	Jungto International Translation Team
Design by	Design Studio Dongkyeong

ISBN: 979-11-87297-46-8 (03220)
Printed in the Republic of Korea.

US $27 ₩20,000

VEN. POMNYUN SUNIM

A Taste of Enlightenment

Stories from Seon Buddhism

JUNGTO

Young man,
when a person sits on a ridge between rice paddies
and keeps one's mind pure,
that person is a practitioner.
And the place where that person sits is a temple.
That is Buddhism.

Your Awakening
Beyond the Awakening of
Seon Masters

There are times when our lives become very complicated, when doing one thing causes a problem somewhere else. The Buddha provides us with a guide to help solve our complicated problems, so we can live a simple and peaceful life.

The Buddha attained enlightenment through his own efforts rather than following someone else's teachings. He tried to rid himself of his own suffering by practicing under several teachers, but he was unable to find the truth through their teachings. That's when the Buddha decided to find his own path to enlightenment. He practiced asceticism for six years but eventually realized it was ineffective for attaining enlightenment. Then, he discovered the Middle Path, which he practiced under the Bodhi tree near the Niranjana River in India. There, he finally attained enlightenment and became free from all suffering and found happiness.

For many years, he wandered in his search for the way to enlightenment before he found the true path. After attaining enlightenment, he realized the path that led to it wasn't that difficult after all. Since he had personally experienced life's suffering, he felt deep sympathy for the countless people who were lost. To end their suffering, he used his own experiences to guide them toward the "Path to Enlightenment."

As the Buddha's teachings spread across much of the world, the practice of Buddhism was influenced by people's hunger to satisfy their worldly desires. As a result, people who practiced Buddhism were not able to relieve their suffering because they couldn't reach enlightenment or nirvana. At that point, there was very little difference between the practice of Buddhism and the practice of any other religion.

To remedy these problems, a new Buddhist movement emerged. Even though it was new, its purpose was to return to the Buddha's fundamental teachings. Eventually, this movement also strayed from the essence of Buddhism and gave rise to another movement aimed at once again returning to the Buddha's original teachings. This repeated rise and fall of movements continues today and has contributed to Buddhism's 2,600-year history.

Today, there are many Buddhist sects in Korea. A mainstream sect, the Jogye Order of Korean Buddhism, descends from Seon Buddhism, a practice that originated in China. Before the rise of Seon Buddhism, Chinese Mahayana Buddhism focused on a difficult and complicated path of scholarly learning rather than guiding its followers toward enlightenment through their own awakening. That's when a movement arose that aimed to solve life's problems in clear and simple ways in accordance with the Buddha's true teachings. Seon Buddhism's slogan became "Pointing directly at one's mind lets one see into one's true nature and attain Buddhahood." This perspective is that one becomes a Buddha by truly understanding one's own nature. In essence, it means that life's problems cannot be resolved through complicated theories or knowledge, so the truth cannot be attained through letters or words. Hence, Seon Buddhism advocates revelation through intuitive insight.

Korean Buddhism succeeded Seon Buddhist traditions. Does that mean Korean Buddhism still follows Seon Buddhism today? If it does, then any Korean Buddhist whose practice is in accordance with the Buddha's teachings should be able to let go of life's problems and experience true freedom and happiness. If they don't experience such freedom and happiness, this tells us that today's Korean Buddhism is far from the Buddha's true teachings even though it is considered Buddhism.

Awakening exists within our lives. Seon dialogues with the Seon masters long ago were about moments of awakening in everyday life. This book examines ways to solve life's problems in clear and simple ways according to the Buddha's teachings. It does this by examining the experience of the great masters throughout Buddhism's 2,600-year history and then looking into our everyday experiences in today's world.

In particular, I want to see if we can really discover the old Seon masters' moments of awakening in our own daily lives and, if we can, find out what is necessary to bring those moments to light. As Buddhism has consistently tried to return to the Dharma, the Buddha's original teachings throughout its history, I would like to find out through my own experiences whether the Buddha's teachings are alive in my everyday life.

Oct., 2022

Ven. Pomnyun Sunim

CONTENTS

PART 01

WHERE ARE YOU RIGHT NOW?

Let's examine the stories of Buddhist monks from long ago with an eye to the problems that cause distress in your life. You need to reflect on your own life since it is useless to try to attain enlightenment by merely referring to other people's stories, as if rummaging through the garbage for their discarded food.

The way to address the problems in your life is to first look at them directly. Then, you'll find that living is really not that complicated. Instead of trying all your life and never experiencing it, if you have an awakening now, you can live the rest of your life enjoying true freedom. Don't make it your goal to practice all your life and only become enlightened right before death. Be awakened now to the way things really are and live the rest of your life happily.

A man asked me, "Sunim*, does heaven exist?"

"Yes, it does."

"Really? Thank you."

But then the same man went to a different monk and repeated his question, "Sunim, does heaven exist?"

"No, it doesn't."

Now the man was confused. He spent hours searching through books looking for the correct answer, but that's not the right way to find the answer. This is like rummaging

---

* A Korean word used to address a Buddhist monk.

through a garbage can full of other people's scraps.

Let's say there is a man wearing a watch and I ask him, "Whose watch is that?"

"It's mine."

"Why is it yours?"

"Because I paid money and bought it."

"Okay, you bought it, but why is it yours?"

"It's mine because I bought it."

"If you pay money and buy something, does it become yours?"

The man keeps insisting the watch is his because he bought it. If I ask one more time, he will get exasperated and say who else could it belong to if not him. No matter what the question is or how earnestly you ask, most people won't be able to take it after the first few times – they will get annoyed or angry. We can't even answer a simple question. That's how obscure our lives are. We struggle with the smallest of things. We act as if we can deal with anything, but when something major happens, when someone we love dies, when we lose our jobs, or when we become bankrupt, we come undone.

For example, suppose you are listening to a Dharma talk

when your phone rings. You put your phone on mute, but this person keeps calling you, so you slip out of the room to take the call. You find out that your mother is dying. In a panic, you leave in the middle of the Dharma talk and rush to the hospital. On the drive there, you're out of your mind with worry. When you arrive at the hospital, your brother calmly informs you that you didn't have to come and that your mother has regained consciousness. Then, you would let out a huge sigh of relief. A few words just sent your emotions on a roller coaster ride.

In another instance, let's say you have your annual physical exam, and the doctor says you need to get more tests done. Right away, your heart starts to pound as though something terrible has already happened. After the additional tests, your doctor says that you need a biopsy, which sends you into a downward spiral.

These examples illustrate how unstable our lives are. It's no different from building castles in the sand. Why is this? It's because we lack conviction about our lives, so we blow this way and that, like leaves in the autumn wind.

There is no one in the world who gets to choose where they will be born. I didn't choose to be born in Korea, to learn to speak Korean, or to eat kimchi. Koreans often say they like kimchi, red pepper paste, or soybean paste, but they didn't choose to like them. Their preferences are simply the result of habits formed over the course of growing up as a Korean.

The people around you attended kindergarten and elementary school, so you naturally follow suit. You go to middle school, high school, and college just like the others do. You also follow the crowd by getting married when others do. Failure to get married by a certain age makes you feel like you are a loser, so you get married, and then you feel compelled to have a child. What you don't know is when you will die or where you'll go after death. People talk about going to heaven or hell after they die, but if you ask them if they've been there themselves, they say, "Someone said so." It's because you let society dictate how to live your life instead of taking hold of the reins that your life feels futile and confusing, like a dream.

Where Did You Come From and Where Are You Going?

When I was a freshman in high school, just like the other students, my biggest wish was to do well in school. At the time, I didn't really know much about the Buddha's teachings, so during an exam period, I would go to the temple to pray that I would get good grades even though I hadn't studied.

One day as I was leaving the Dharma Hall, the temple abbot called me over. His request made me anxious because I knew once he started talking, he would go on and on for hours. When I would think he was done, I'd stand up, and then he would continue talking for another hour. On that day, I had an exam I had to study for that was coming up the next day. I'd been thinking of pulling an all-nighter when he intercepted me on my way out of the temple. Before he could say anything, I said, "Sunim, I'm busy today." I thought that if I told him I was busy, he would let me go right away.

"Is that so?" he asked. For a second, I thought I'd escaped one of his long lectures, but then he suddenly began asking me a series of rather odd questions. "Where did you come from?" he asked.

"From the library."

"Where did you come from before the library?"

"From school."

"What about before school?"

"From home."

"And before that?"

He continued with his nonsensical questions until I got to the point where my answer was "I was born."

"Where were you born from?"

"From my mother's womb."

"Where did you come from before your mother's womb?"

"I don't know, Sunim," I answered because I really didn't know.

"Is that so?" There was a moment of silence before he asked, "Where are you going?"

"I'm going to the school library."

"And after that?"

"To school tomorrow to take an exam."

"And after the exam?"

"Back home."

"And after that?"

"I'll come to the temple."

We continued in this fashion for a while until I answered, "I will die."

"And after dying?"

"I don't know."

Once again, I had no clue, so I said so.

That's when he suddenly bellowed at me: "You, boy, why are you so busy when you don't even know where you came from or where you're going?"

Up to that point, my answers had been half-hearted because I thought his questions were pointless, but his last words shook me to the core.

He wanted to know how I could be busy when I didn't even know where I came from or where I was going. Why had my first impulse been to cut him off? When he called me, I should have responded, "Sunim, did you call me? What is it?" I should have first listened to what he had to say before explaining my situation to him. However, I was caught up in my own thoughts and didn't consider him at all. So, when he called me, I told him right away, "I'm busy." And then, to his questions about where I came from and where I was going, I said, "I don't know," as if this was something to be proud of. Then, of course, as he pointed out, how could I be busy when I didn't know where I came from and where I was going? It's a contradiction.

The reason I eventually left home to live at the temple was not that I wanted to be a monk or seek blessings. It was because I wanted to know the answer to the question of where I came from and where I was going.

You and I, all lead busy lives. But why are we busy? Do we know where we are going and why we are going there?

Can You Attain Enlightenment Through Sitting Meditation?

Buddhism can be characterized by its simplicity, clarity, and transparency. Our lives are made complicated by the affliction stemming from our own ignorance. It's like someone who is sleeping in a comfortable bed but suffers from nightmares all night. Once we are able to awaken from our nightmares, we will be at peace. This is Buddhism.

The essence of Buddhism is clear and simple. However, during the extended period of time that it was being disseminated, Buddhism became unnecessarily complicated. Therefore, Seon Buddhism redefined Buddhism so that people could approach the truth in a direct, clear, and simple way. Buddhism values awakening, which leads to freedom from all struggles and constraints. Seon Buddhism, in particular, places emphasis on such awakening.

The following story about the practice of Seon Buddhism illustrates this point. There was a monk who was in the middle of practicing sitting meditation when his teacher walked by. The teacher stopped and asked him what he was doing. The disciple thought it an odd question since this was the teacher who had instructed him in the practice. In any event, he gave a straightforward answer, "I am doing sitting meditation, Sunim." The teacher then asked, "Why are you practicing sitting meditation?" The disciple politely answered, "To attain enlightenment." The teacher tilted his head and said, "Really?" Then, he walked away.

The disciple thought it was strange that a teacher would disturb his own disciple's deep meditative state for no apparent reason. This interaction left his mind unsettled, but eventually, the disciple was once again able to enter into a deep meditative state. But shortly after, he was disturbed by a scraping noise. When he could no longer ignore the sound, he glanced out of the corner of his eyes and saw his teacher sitting next to him, rubbing two bricks against each other. Now the disciple felt perplexed, wondering what on earth his teacher was doing. He just had to ask, "Teacher, what are you doing?"

"I am making a mirror."

Without thinking, the disciple blurted out, "How is it possible to make a mirror by rubbing two bricks together?"

Before the disciple had even finished his question, the teacher roared, "How is it possible to attain enlightenment by practicing sitting meditation?"

What is the meaning of this story? The point is that practicing sitting meditation in order to attain enlightenment is as useless as rubbing two bricks together in order to make a mirror. The disciple believed he was doing the right thing by following his teacher's guidance, only to have his teacher scold him for doing something the teacher now said was pointless. With complete sincerity, the disciple asked, "Then what should I do to attain enlightenment?"

The teacher replied, "If you are steering an oxcart and the cart stops, which one should you whip, the ox or the cart?"

It is said that the disciple attained enlightenment upon hearing this.

However, there is another version of this story that says the disciple did not attain enlightenment at that moment, but instead, answered, "I would whip the ox." At this point, the teacher shouted, "Then, why are you whipping the cart?" In this version, it is said that the disciple attained enlightenment at the very moment his teacher scolded him.

This is a very famous dialogue between Nanyue Huairang and Mazu Daoyi, who were both great Seon masters. Instead of focusing on the formalities, you need to see through to the essence of the matter. That is Seon in a nutshell.

You can't practice Seon by merely following someone else's lead. Seon does not exist in the process of sitting down. The Buddha does not take a constant form. The Dharma cannot be explained using one framework or another. It is only attainable by experiencing it with your own mind, and this cannot be achieved by blindly practicing certain forms. The Buddha said the truth cannot be verified by sutras, doctrines, knowledge, habits, customs, ethics, or morals transmitted from the past.

Then, how do we prove the truth today? Typically, we say it was in such-and-such a sutra (an aphorism from ancient texts) or so-and-so's dissertation, or that we saw it in the encyclopedia or in the newspaper. Also, we say that this monk or that pastor said it, that it was in the Bible, or that it's been this way since ages ago. That is, we try to verify the truth by using something outside of ourselves as evidence.

But the truth cannot be verified that way. It can only be verified through intuitive discernment. That does not mean you don't need words. It means that the truth cannot be transmitted through words. Simply put, words cannot be considered absolute. You have to let go of your attachment to external things, and then focus your mind on the truth. You need to experience it yourself. Only then can you become rock solid in your practice.

There was a monk who visited an eminent teacher and asked him, "What is the way to enlightenment?" The eminent monk answered, "Chang-Cheong Chang-Cheong." This bizarre reply rendered the visiting monk speechless, so he went to his own teacher. He told his teacher that he had asked the eminent monk what is the way to enlightenment, and the monk had replied, "Chang-Cheong Chang-Cheong." He added that he had no idea what it meant.

"Is that so? What did you say back to him?"

"I couldn't think of anything to say."

"Then, go back and ask him the same question, and if

he gives you the same answer, say 'Ahem' and see what happens."

So, the monk returned to the eminent teacher and once again asked, "What is the way to enlightenment?" He waited for the same answer, "Chang-Cheong Chang-Cheong," so he could say, "Ahem." But guess what? The monk answered, "Ahem." Once again, the monk was left speechless.

As this story suggests, enlightenment cannot be attained by copying someone else's thoughts or actions. Nor is it something you can achieve by following anyone else's guidance. If you study the dialogues of the Seon masters and decide that when you are asked a question, you can simply copy the master's words, you are wrong. Their answers are dead phrases when outside a particular context. When the original teachings of the Buddha were shaped into Buddhist doctrines, Mahayana Buddhism criticized the doctrines as blind adherence to the Dharma. When Mahayana Buddhism, in turn, became ideological, Seon Buddhism broke free with the concept of revelation through intuitive discernment. Now Seon Buddhism is becoming formalized. Enlightenment cannot be attained by imitating forms.

That you should not be bound by a specific framework

does not mean that all forms need to be thrown away. Being free of form can also mean using form when necessary. The statement that Seon Buddhism does not exist in sitting meditation means that you cannot get into a Seon state of mind simply by sitting. On the other hand, this doesn't mean that sitting meditation cannot get you into a Seon frame of mind. If you misinterpret these teachings, it is easy to become skewed to one side.

There Are No Blessings
to Be Attained

The founder of Seon Buddhism, also known as the first patriarch, was Bodhidharma who arrived in China from India. Bodhidharma did not claim that he wanted to start Seon Buddhism. However, when we look back at how Seon Buddhism was established, it is evident that Seon Buddhism began with Bodhidharma. That is why he is called the first master of Seon Buddhism. The second master was Huike; the third, Sengcan; the fourth, Daoxin; the fifth, Hongren; the sixth, Huineng, the seventh, Nanyue Huairang; and the eighth, Mazu Daoyi.

When Bodhidharma first arrived in China, it was governed

by the Northern and Southern Dynasties, with the Liang Dynasty located south of the Yangtze River. Emperor Wu, the founder of the Liang Dynasty, was a devout Buddhist who generously supported Buddhism. He contributed significantly to Buddhism's growth by constructing hundreds of temples and translating, publishing, and distributing numerous Buddhist sutras. Buddhist monks at the time praised him by comparing him to a Chakravartin, which translates to the king of kings or ideal ruler. In India, one of the greatest Indian kings, King Asoka, was considered a Chakravartin. So, if India had King Asoka, China had Emperor Wu.

When Emperor Wu learned that an eminent monk was visiting from India, he invited Bodhidharma to his palace. Upon meeting him, Emperor Wu explained the state of Buddhism in Liang and told Bodhidharma that he, himself, had built hundreds of temples, translated and distributed tens of thousands of Buddhist sutras, and educated thousands of monks. It was a great achievement. After explaining this, the emperor asked the Venerable Bodhidharma how much merit he had earned.

The purpose of his question was to have an eminent

"Who are you?"
"I don't know."

monk attest to the blessings that would be coming his way. According to Buddhist sutras, the merit of doing anything for Buddhism is so great that just drawing the face of the Buddha in the sand or building a pagoda out of sand just for fun would form a karmic affinity that would enable one to attain enlightenment. So, Emperor Wu wondered how enormous his merit would be. Bodhidharma answered, "None."

Bodhidharma not only saw through Emperor Wu's words but also had the courage to state it out loud. Even though Emperor Wu was a devout Buddhist, he was deeply irritated by Bodhidharma's words, especially after all the work he'd done for Buddhism. It would have been better if the emperor had looked into his own mind the moment he became irritated, but he didn't.

Bodhidharma's answer puzzled him. He wondered what the Four Noble Truths, one of the greatest teachings of the Buddha, meant if everything he had done had not earned him any merit. He was convinced that he'd accumulated limitless merit because he had given so much to Buddhism. He believed that building temples, distributing Buddhist sutras, and educating monks were the way to realize the highest ideal of Buddhism. He was upset by Bodhidharma's words but also curious. So, he asked, "What is the first noble truth?" Bodhidharma answered, "There is nothing to be called noble because it is empty." Then, Emperor Wu asked, "Who are you?" meaning, "Who are you to say such a thing to me?" And Bodhidharma answered, "I don't know."

Bodhidharma's answer infuriated the emperor and he pulled out his sword to behead the monk. Thankfully, he was stopped just in time by the other monks who were present. Even though Emperor Wu was praised for being a devout Buddhist, he attempted to kill a distinguished monk just because he said something the emperor didn't like. At a moment like this, we have to look at the mind and emotions arising within ourselves. If we only look outside of ourselves rather than looking inward, we will be blinded by our anger.

Bodhidharma traveled around Liang but saw nothing that reflected the Buddha's teachings. There were magnificent temples, countless sutras, and numerous monks in fine robes, but the Dharma, the Buddha's teachings, was not alive. So, he crossed the Yangtze River and wandered north into a sparsely populated area and eventually settled down at the Shaolin Temple. Nevertheless, when word traveled that a famous monk from India was visiting, renowned scholars came from all over China to see him. They arrived with all sorts of questions and asked for all sorts of favors. They implored that he teach them martial arts, ways to get supernatural powers, or Sanskrit. However, no one was interested in learning about non-attachment, one of the Buddha's core teachings.

There is a phrase in the *Heart Sutra*: "There is no wisdom and there is no attainment because there is nothing to be attained." It means there is nothing to call enlightenment or no way to attain enlightenment because there is nothing to be attained. However, people who had recited the *Heart Sutra* countless times and had attended Buddhist temples for several decades were not interested in the Buddha's teachings. All sorts of people came only to try and gain worldly things. As a result, no matter what they asked for or said, Bodhidharma remained silent.

Bring Forth Your Uneasy Mind

For nine years, Bodhidharma turned his face to a wall, refusing to speak a word. He had come to spread the Dharma, but no one was seeking it. All they desired were selfish and worldly things. The people who had come to get something from him quickly left because he gave them no reason to stay. For years, people continued to come and go like the ebb and flow of the tides.

Only one monk continued to stay. When Bodhidharma meditated, this monk meditated. When Bodhidharma worked, he worked. When Bodhidharma performed the daily ceremony, he attended it. One winter day after

Bodhidharma finished meditating, he came out of the temple and noticed this monk meditating in the snow. Bodhidharma opened his mouth for the first time in nine years to ask, "Why did you come? All sorts of people have traveled here in an attempt to get all kinds of things, but they soon left. So, what have you been waiting for all these years?" The monk told Bodhidharma that he had come to find the way to attain peace and enlightenment.

So, Bodhidharma asked, "How is your mind right now?" The monk said, "My mind is very uneasy. Please make my uneasy mind become more at ease." Imagine how desperate he must have felt when the Bodhidharma finally showed an interest in him after waiting for nine years.

Bodhidharma replied, "Is that so? Bring forth your uneasy mind, and I will put it at ease." Now all he had to do was say, "Here it is!" and show Bodhidharma his uneasy mind. Would he find it in his knapsack? In the Buddhist sutras? No, he needed to look inward, inside himself.

This is what teachers do. Until that moment, the disciple had been searching for answers outside himself. He thought the truth existed external to himself and came to meet the teacher despite the long distance over rough roads. But this

A Taste of Enlightenment

dialogue made him turn his eyes inward. If he wanted to bring forth his mind, he couldn't find it outside himself.

A long silence followed Bodhidharma's words. It was the silence of the monk looking into his own mind. After some time, the disciple said, "There is nothing for me to bring forth." And the teacher said, "Then, I have already put your mind at ease."

Was the disciple's mind put at ease when the teacher told him he put it at ease? Or was it already at ease when the disciple said there was nothing for him to bring forth? The teacher did not give him enlightenment; the disciple enlightened himself. You can't give or take enlightenment. The one who attained enlightenment in this manner was the Venerable Huike, the second patriarch of Seon Buddhism.

Grave Sin

Huike became famous as a great teacher who passed on the true Dharma. One night, at the temple where he lived as the abbot, a man came to his room. The man was a leper desperately searching for the way to enlightenment. At the time, leprosy was incurable and contagious. Anyone who contracted the disease was exiled to a remote hut where food would be delivered until they died. If a leper came down to a village to beg for food, people would turn away in fear of contracting the disease. Lepers were totally shunned, not only by their families but also by the rest of society. Leprosy was thought to be a punishment from the heavens. People believed that an inflicted person's sins were so heavy that the heavens punished them with the disease.

Huike's visitor was the son of a noble family and, at one time, a government official, but he had been isolated from the world since becoming a leper. Imagine how traumatic that must have been for him. Most lepers subsisted on begging until they died, but this man was an intellectual. He believed that while he might be punished by the heavens in this world and die as a leper, he needed to have his sins forgiven, so he wouldn't continue to suffer in his next life. When he heard there was a renowned monk in the area, he desperately wanted to visit him to find a way to have his sins forgiven. As lepers were not allowed to enter a temple, he wrapped his deformed face and hands in cloth and, in the darkness of night, knocked on the door of the temple's abbot. Huike only realized the man was a leper after he had invited him into his room.

The leper lowered his eyes and prostrated himself. "Venerable master, please forgive these grave sins of mine." He desperately wanted to have his sins forgiven because he believed his illness was heaven's punishment. Huike, realizing the man prostrated before him was educated, replied, "Bring forth your grave sin and I will forgive them."

It was a heaven-sent opportunity. All the leper had to do was bring forth the grave sins he was carrying on his shoulders. How would he bring them forth? Did he have to return to his hut to search for them? Would he find them in the sky? Or did he have to dig in the ground for them? No, all he had to do was look within himself. This is what teachers do. They help you turn your eyes inward.

A long silence ensued. He was on the brink of getting his most profound wish fulfilled. Think about how desperately he must have been searching for a way to relieve this heaviness he'd been carrying in his heart, wanting to unburden himself of what he thought were grave sins. Finally, after a long time had passed, he said, "There is nothing for me to bring forth." And the teacher told him, "Then, I have already forgiven your sins."

What Is This Thing That Came?

The greatest among Huineng's disciples was Nanyue Huairang, the seventh master. He became a monk with the goal of attaining enlightenment, and, in search of that goal, he spent ten years studying under various teachers. A teacher he met on Mt. Songshan advised him to visit Huineng. So, he braved the long distance and rough roads for many days. He arrived at the temple soaked in sweat. With a pounding heart, he opened the door of the teacher's room to introduce himself. However, the minute he set foot in the room, Huineng roared like thunder, "What is this thing that came?"

He froze on the spot. It was true he had come, but he could not think of an answer to "What is this thing?" It wasn't a corpse that had come, so he couldn't say his body came. It was not his name that had come, so he couldn't say so-and-so came either. He couldn't open his mouth.

The question, "What is this thing that came?" is the same as asking, "Who are you?" It's a fact that your physical presence has come, but if you don't know who you are, there's no use asking any more questions. How can someone who doesn't know who he is ask questions? Nanyue Huairang awkwardly stood with one foot inside the room and the other foot outside the room. He then quietly closed the door and left without saying goodbye. He had traveled such a long distance to meet this teacher but had to leave without saying a word.

It took him seven years to find the answer to that question, "Who am I?" Whether he answered that question immediately, after a while, or seven years later, it doesn't make much of a difference. Some versions of this story skip the seven-year part and say he answered right away. Anyway, as described in other versions of this story, he came back after seven years, bowed to the teacher, and said, "Teacher, to call

it a thing is not right. It is something you can't call a thing."
Hearing this, the teacher asked him, "Is it something that
needs to be cleaned?" "You can say you clean it; however,
you can't make it dirty."

You can say you clean it, but it's not inherently dirty, so
you can't make it dirty. There is nothing to be angry, pained,
or sad about; it is what it is. All phenomena are simply what
they are. They are pure, not in the sense of being the opposite
of dirty, but they are fundamentally neither clean nor dirty.
That is the true nature of all phenomena. But from time to
time, we become confused and deluded. We see things as
if they are a mirage in the desert or a phantom in a dream
when, in reality, there's nothing there. That is why we need
to maintain mindfulness and remain awake at all times. We
need to be aware each time a feeling or thought arises in
response to an external phenomenon that stirs us like waves
rising in the sea. Only then will we avoid being swept away
by the waves.

There are times when life feels difficult and painful. At those times, we need to see through our afflictions rather than get lost in them. We need to quickly wake up from the nightmare.

If you live alone, it should feel good to live alone. If you live with someone, it should feel good to live with someone. If you have a child, it should be nice to have a child. And if you don't, that should feel good as well. If you trip over a stone in the street, you need to get up, find a shovel, and remove it, preventing any more people from tripping over it. At that point, the fact that you tripped over a stone today becomes a wonderful thing. If you hadn't tripped, you wouldn't have noticed the obstacle. Tripping over the stone turned out to be a blessing in disguise.

Anything that happens in this world is simply an incident. An incident, in itself, is neither a disaster nor a blessing. It is up to us to turn it into one or the other. Everything depends on your mind and perspective. You can turn any incident in your life into a disaster. You can lament, "Oh, poor me! This is just my luck. What sin did I commit in my previous life to suffer like this?" But you are the one who made it into a disaster. Instead, you can turn things around so that everything becomes a blessing. Practicing the Dharma is about making yourself and your life blessed and beautiful. Buddhism teaches you to change your destiny rather than passively accept it. You can change your fate. Dharma practice can liberate you from the grip of the destiny shared by all living creatures, which is to be born over and over again in the six realms of samsaric existence, the cycles of conditioned existence, birth and death, perpetuating suffering. This is why you need to practice.

You don't have to be a Buddhist to learn the Dharma and follow the path of practice. Whether or not you have a religion is of little consequence. Dharma transcends all things, including religion, status, gender, etc. Anyone can attain enlightenment if they practice according to the Dharma. It doesn't matter if you belong to a different religion or sect. Our constitution protects our freedom of religion, so there is no need to change your religion. The important thing is that, regardless of your religion, anyone who engages in Dharma practices can be truly free and happy.

In their daily lives, some Buddhist scholars, who teach Buddhism, fight with their wives or have problems with their children. Even monks, who return to lay life and get married and have children, become annoyed with their wives and children. Why is that? Because they haven't experienced the truth. You can acquire all the forms that make you appear enlightened on the surface, but if you haven't actually experienced the Dharma directly through your own experience, then they won't be helpful in your life.

Many members of the Jungto Society, the community of practitioners I founded, are not Buddhists. This is especially true among overseas members of the Jungto Society. About half of them have other religions, mostly Christianity. I often give Dharma talks to church-goers. However, if I invite

Christians to come to a Buddhist temple, they won't come, so I hold my talks in restaurants or auditoriums, and I talk about general concerns rather than Buddhism. I can't tell people who attend church on Sunday and attend a Dharma talk on another day to stop going to church and start going to a temple. I don't need to tell people what to do. I just focus on delivering this wonderful Dharma. There are people who study Buddhism while believing in other religions, and there are people who change their religion to Buddhism once they start to study the Dharma. It is up to the individual.

I hope that Christians and non-believers will listen regularly to my Dharma talks. Non-believers are ideal candidates for studying the Dharma since they don't believe in a particular faith and tend to be skeptical and ask a lot of questions. They can easily solve their problems by exchanging a few words with me. Religious people are more difficult, and Buddhists are the hardest. They delude themselves that because they attend a temple, they know the Dharma. Even though a person faithfully attends a temple for religious purposes, that person still needs to study the Dharma. I'm talking about the kind of regimen that focuses on the way to attain the state of enlightenment that lies beyond religion and science

— the path to true happiness and freedom.

It is all right if your spouse or your parents don't like the fact that you're studying the Dharma. Did Princess Yasodhara, the Buddha's wife, and King Suddhodana, the Buddha's father, like it when the Buddha left home? No, they did not. You shouldn't be swayed by what your wife, husband, or parents say. They cannot be your guide in life. Parents can't help their children attain enlightenment because their primary goal is to keep their children safe. Even Confucius, a great philosopher, was probably just another annoying husband to his wife.

Remember that how you view your wife, your husband, or your child is not necessarily right. My father told me, "What good is it to be respected by other people? You don't even have a child of your own. Even the grass in the field spreads its seeds." The standard that parents use to measure their children against is very different from the standard that other people use. If you listen to your parents at all times, it will be difficult for you to find and follow the right path. You can't listen to your spouse at all times either. This doesn't mean you should ignore them. It simply means that when you are following the path to the truth, it is up to you to awaken to what the truth is. Without this awakening, you won't know what to do or who to listen to.

You need to look directly at your own problems in order to solve them. Then, your life will no longer be complicated. It isn't true that you won't be able to solve your problems until you die, no matter how hard you try. You can solve them now and live in freedom for the rest of your life. Don't aim to practice and study so you attain enlightenment just before you die. Attain enlightenment in the here and now, so you may live in happiness for the rest of your life.

PART 02

DO YOU KNOW YOURSELF?

We don't realize that we are imprisoned by our thoughts. Even if the Buddha came to the current world, we wouldn't recognize him. Even if there was a great teacher, we wouldn't hear what they are saying. This is neither the fault of the teacher nor the Buddha. Unless we open our own eyes, no matter how many Buddhas come to this world, they cannot help us. So, stop blaming others and focus on looking inward and opening your eyes.

How Can There Be Relics from a Wooden Buddha?

Many years ago, a monk spent 10 years diligently practicing with the goal of seeing the Buddha and attaining enlightenment. He was praised by everyone for his unswerving practice, but he never saw the Buddha, the embodiment of the Dharma.

This monk thought to himself, "I am going to pray really hard for three years even if it kills me. If I still haven't seen the Buddha at the end of the three years, it might be better for me to return to lay life, be a filial son to my parents, and be useful in the world."

With his reaffirmed aspiration of seeing the Buddha, he traveled to a small temple on a remote mountain. He did not leave that mountain for three years. He prayed and made offerings to the Buddha four times every day. In the winter of his third year, when the last day of his thousand-day prayer was quickly approaching, he began to feel impatient because he still had not attained enlightenment. That winter, it snowed heavily, and eventually, he could no longer find firewood or go down the mountain to the village to collect food given to him as alms by the local people.

When he ran out of both, he headed out early one morning to obtain food and fuel to ease his hunger and cold. He barely managed to reach the village through the snowy trail. While he was making his alms round, a blizzard hit the mountain, preventing him from returning to the temple. He was terribly anxious to get back in time to complete the final day of his thousand-day prayer. Every day for almost a thousand days, he'd prayed and made offerings to the Buddha. Would this snowstorm cause him to fail to reach his goal? But no matter how anxious he became, the snowstorm raged on. A week passed while he waited helplessly for the snow to stop falling.

Finally, it stopped, and he set out for the mountain, determined to get to the temple even if he died in the attempt. He stumbled and struggled through the deep snow until he finally reached the small temple. He was catching his breath when he noticed a pair of unfamiliar straw shoes by the doorway. Although he was not expecting a visitor, it was evident that someone had come. The person could not have arrived during the snowstorm because he had seen no footprints in the snow on his way back up the mountain. So, he thought it was most likely that the visitor had arrived the same day he'd left a week earlier. With the temple lacking both fuel and food, he worried that the person might have frozen to death. He'd left the temple before he had completed his thousand-day prayer, had missed making his offerings to the Buddha, and now he felt responsible for the death of another human being. Seized with regret, he opened the door to his room, where he found his visitor snoring away on the warm floor. He was relieved that the man was still alive but wondered where he'd found the fuel to heat the room. Although he found the situation puzzling, he decided he would pay respect to the Buddha before talking to his visitor.

"Dear Lord Buddha, I am sorry I haven't made offerings for a week due to my lack of devotion." He prostrated himself before the Buddha, repenting his wrongdoing, and raised his head to discover the statue of the Buddha was missing. A thought hit him like a bolt of lightning: "That scoundrel burned the Buddha!"

He ran back to the room, flung open the door, grabbed the man by his collar, and shouted, "Damn you! No matter how cold you were, how could you burn the Buddha? You're a monk!" He was furious. The Buddha that the visitor had burned wasn't just any Buddha. It was the Buddha he'd prayed to for almost one thousand days. The visiting monk said, "Sunim, let go of me for a moment. I have something to show you, so please let go of me."

The small temple was surrounded by snow so deep there was no place for the other monk to hide if he tried to run away, so the angry monk released the other man, who quickly ran out of the room. He followed the other monk, only to discover him rummaging through the ashes in the furnace with a fire poker. He asked, "What on earth are you doing? Why are you combing through the ashes?"

The visiting monk answered, "I'm searching for the Buddha's relics." What he meant was that since he'd cremated the Buddha, there should be sacred relics, like bone fragments, in the ashes. The monk was dumbfounded. "You rascal, how can a wooden Buddha leave relics behind?" The visiting monk who was still holding the poker replied, "Well, I will go and get the rest to feed the furnace." At that moment, the monk attained enlightenment.

The monk had been furious because he thought the visiting monk had burned the Buddha. But when the visiting monk said he was looking for relics, the angry monk asked how there could be relics from a wooden Buddha. How could a block of wood be the Buddha? It was nothing more than a block of wood.

Just moments before, he'd been furious. He'd attacked the visiting monk and demanded to know how he could have burned the Buddha. What he hadn't realized was the contradiction inherent in his words. When he asked how a wooden Buddha could produce relics, the visiting monk told him that he would burn the rest. He meant, "Why would you enshrine a wooden statue in the Buddha Hall and worship it instead of burning it to stay warm?" That's when the monk realized the contradiction, and he was released from the trap of his own thoughts.

This is enlightenment – experiencing a new world opening up in that instant. If the monk had really burned the Buddha, there would have been sacred relics in the ashes. But how could a wooden Buddha produce relics? It couldn't be because it was not the Buddha; it was just a block of wood. This is a famous koan (a riddle or puzzle on which you meditate in Seon practice to demonstrate the inadequacy of logical reasoning and provoke doubt): "How can there be relics from a wooden Buddha?" It is one of the stories about how great Buddhist teachers attained enlightenment.

We are often full of contradictions like this, but we don't recognize it. This not knowing is ignorance. There are times when we know something but don't practice what we know. But there are also times when we simply do not know. When you ask an angry person why they are angry, the answer often is, "Who says I'm angry?" And when you tell someone who is drinking that they're very drunk, they'll answer, "No, I'm perfectly sober." If that person had answered, "You think so? Am I really drunk?" it would mean that they're not that drunk. The person who knows they are drunk is less intoxicated compared to the person who doesn't even realize how drunk they are. The person who is angry but becomes aware of their feelings may think, "Oh, I've gotten all angry." They may still be angry at that moment, but they can find a way to free themselves from it. However, the person who doesn't even recognize that they are angry and asks, "Who says I'm angry?" can't find a way to escape it.

We are not aware of our own ignorance. Forget about how to address the root of the problem; we don't even realize that we're full of ignorance. Sometimes, we do something wrong, but we don't even know we did. We are incorrect but don't know it. We think to ourselves that everything is fine, but strangely enough, we feel troubled and sad inside. In our hearts, there is a constant barrage of worries, anxieties, fears, and resentment.

During a five-day Awakening Retreat* run by the Jungto Society, there was a woman who said that, throughout her entire marriage, she had never admitted to her husband that she was wrong. I asked her how that was possible, and she replied that it was because she had never done anything wrong. However, her husband had asked me, "If my wife comes here and practices for several days, will she become a decent human being?" During the entire retreat, she never reflected on her own behavior, not even once. But on the last day, she said to me, "Sunim, I'm a little stubborn, aren't I?"

Although she hadn't experienced an awakening, she sensed

---

* Awakening Retreat is a five-day retreat during which a Dharma teacher guides the participants to look into their minds and experience awakening.

from the way others acted around her that there might be something wrong with her. Even this small insight can change one's life. Several days later, the woman's older sister called me and asked, "Sunim, what did you do to my sister? She's become a different person after attending the Awakening Retreat."

Knowing yourself is of prime importance. Whether you can change yourself or not, or whether you know yourself a lot or a little, the first step is to know yourself as you truly are. You need to know you're wrong when you're wrong so that you can fix it. You need to know you made a mistake when you make a mistake, so you can learn from it. You need to know when you don't know something so that you can learn about it. If you don't even know that you don't know, there is no hope for change. This is ignorance, the root of all suffering.

Who Made God?

Nowadays, there are volunteers who drive me to the places where I give Dharma talks. But in the past, I used to take public transportation. One day, while I was waiting at Seoul Station for a train to Busan to attend a Dharma meeting, two young men approached me, both in black suits and ties and each carrying a black briefcase. They greeted me politely, and I thought they were very cordial young men. Then, out of the blue, one of them asked me, "Sir, who do you think made the things in this station?"

I didn't answer. I couldn't figure out why they were asking me such a nonsensical question. Since I wasn't saying anything, the young man asked me again, "Surely, all the things in this station were made by someone, don't you think?"

"Well, yes, I suppose someone made them," I said.

"Then, who made this world?"

I still couldn't figure out where this conversation was headed, so again I said nothing.

Once again, he asked, "If there is nothing in this station that was not made by someone, this world must have been made by someone, right?"

So, I said, "Do things always have to be made? Some things are made, some things occur naturally, and some have existed from the beginning. There are many possibilities." I thought this was the logical answer.

The young man spoke again. "How can you say that? Did the electricity in this station appear naturally or did someone make it? Did this column appear naturally, or did someone make it? Each of these things was made by someone. How could all of creation and all the wonderful, different things in the world occur naturally? All things were made by someone. Who made them?"

As I remained silent while the two young men pressured

"Who made this world?"
"God, the creator, made it."
"Then, who made God?"
"What?"

me, people began gathering around us. They thought the two young men had cornered a monk who couldn't come up with an answer to their question, "Who made this world?"

After a brief moment, I asked them, "Do all things in this world need to be made by someone? Isn't there anything that existed from the start or that occurred naturally?"

"Of course not."

They insisted there was nothing that was not made by someone. I asked them if there were any exceptions and they said there were no exceptions. So, I asked, "Who made this world?"

"God, our Creator, made it."

"I see. Then, who made God?"

"What?"

"I asked, who made God?"

"He existed from the beginning."

"You just told me there is nothing that existed from the beginning. So, who made God?"

Now, it was the young men who couldn't answer. They would ask people if they knew who made this world, and when people couldn't answer, they would tell them that God made it. Probably it was the first time that they were then asked, "Who made God?" They had never thought about it, so they couldn't answer my question.

Eventually, the time came for me to get on the train. As I picked up my luggage, I whispered to them, so no one else could overhear, "You made God, didn't you?"

The point of this story is not about slandering a particular religion. I'm telling you this story, so we can examine the ways that humans get caught up in their own thoughts. We are entangled in our beliefs and only think from that point of view. However, if we look from another point of view, things are completely different. People insist on their own beliefs and their own point of view, claiming they are right and others are wrong, that they know and others don't, and that they are good and others are bad.

Making Rice with Sand

A while back, I attended an international Buddhist conference in the United States. Most of the participants were professors of Buddhist Studies, who taught Buddhism at universities. I asked them what was the most difficult thing about teaching Buddhism, and their answer was that it was talking about the creation of the universe. In Christianity, it is believed that God created the universe. So, when Christians ask them who created this world, the professors found themselves unable to answer based on what they knew of Buddhist teachings. They knew this was the result of the different ways of thinking between the two religions but still didn't know how to explain it to the students.

I told them to ask me the question.

"Who created this world?"

I kept silent.

"Is silence the answer?" they asked.

So, I asked them, "How many hours would it take to make steamed rice with sand?"

"What?"

"How long does it take to make steamed rice with sand?"

"You can't make rice with sand."

"I didn't ask you if you could make rice with sand. I asked you how many hours it takes to make rice from sand."

"What?"

"How long?"

"Oh, I understand."

When I ask, "How many hours would it take to make steamed rice with sand?" in response to the question, "In Buddhism, who created this world?" sensible people understand right away. One hour, 10 hours, 100 hours… none of these are the right answers. The question itself is wrong to begin with. People who don't understand this get caught up in the words, wrestling with the question to figure out how many hours it would take.

On the other hand, those who clearly understand that the question itself is nonsensical don't get tricked by the words. They answer, "You can't make steamed rice with sand." Even though the question wasn't about whether you can make steamed rice with sand, it's meaningless to discuss how long it would take if it's impossible to make steamed rice with sand in the first place.

When you ask people who created the world, they try to think "who" and answer, but the question presumes that this world was, indeed, created. The question, how long does it take to make steamed rice with sand, also presumes that you can make steamed rice with sand. However, the premise is wrong. Being asked the question, "Who created the world?" traps us within the premise that the world was created. You become confused because you can't see through the fact that the premise itself is incorrect. It's like getting the question, "How many hours would it take to make steamed rice from sand?" and then doing all kinds of research by searching through encyclopedias for the answer. There is no need to research it in the first place since the question is based on an incorrect premise. The question, "Who created this world?"

presupposes that someone created it in the first place. There is no evidence that this world was created. We keep silent about such questions not because we don't know the answer, but because the question sounds like someone mumbling in their sleep. It's nonsense; there is no need to answer it. I don't mean to criticize any religion in particular. My point is that we need to reflect on how often our starting point is based on an incorrect premise.

When a woman complains that her husband's drinking drives her crazy, her complaint is based on the premise that drinking is bad. She tries to change her spouse based on that premise. But her husband doesn't accept that premise. If she prays based on the premise that drinking is bad, her prayer won't be answered no matter how long or hard she prays. However, if you abandon that premise, you can see the essence of the problem.

"Buddha, please make my husband drink a lot." If you pray this way, your problem will be resolved immediately. After 30 years of not answering your prayers, Buddha will instantly respond, and your problem will be solved.

We wander this way and that based on an incorrect premise, which is why our problems in life persist no matter how hard we try. We have to see things in a new light by changing our perspectives and fixed ways of thinking.

Is Cow Dung Sacred or Dirty?

This story takes place in the village of Durgapur, located near the Dungeshwari Caves in Bodh Gaya in Bihar, India, where the Buddha practiced asceticism for six years. The residents of Durgapur are known as "Dalits." Twenty years ago, only two out of the 1,300 residents living in the three neighboring villages had graduated from primary school. These people were living in poverty, making a daily wage of less than a dollar a day, and there was not enough food, water, or clothing. They couldn't even afford medical treatment if they became sick.

I made a commitment to build a school and a hospital in

this village. The villagers provided the land, and every day, 30 to 40 residents came to work on the building. I lived and worked with them. We dug the foundation, laid the bricks, and put up concrete columns. The villagers lived in mud huts that were dark inside even during the day because there weren't any windows. At night, they slept on the bare dirt floor or on straw mats, like their domestic animals.

One day, after finishing work, I returned to the place where I was staying. The yard and floor of my hut had a greenish tinge and an odd smell. When I looked closely, I could tell that the yard and floor had been painted with something, which had dried. Pointing at the floor, I asked the landlord, "What is this?"

"Oh! We cleaned the house and made it sacred, especially for you,"

"I see. Thank you. But what is this?"

"It's cow dung."

"What? Cow dung? You painted the floor with cow dung?"

"Yes. When an important guest comes or when we perform Pooja,* we clean the house and then paint it with cow dung

---

* Pooja is a Hindu ceremonial worship, ranging from brief daily rites in the home to elaborate temple rituals.

diluted with water."

"Really? You welcome important guests by painting the house with cow dung? That is how you make the house sacred? With the dirty cow dung?"

"Did you say that cow dung is dirty?"

"Of course cow dung is dirty. How can it be clean? No matter how sacred the cow is, cow dung is still dung, isn't it? Humans are precious, but does this make human dung precious?"

"What do you mean it's dirty? How can it be dirty? It's the fuel we use to cook our food, the kindling we use to light a fire, and the incense we use to produce smoke during sacred rituals. It's not dirty dung."

"What do you mean it's not dung?"

"What do you mean it's dung? It's fertilizer, medicine, fuel, and incense."

"?......!"

There is a mountain. The people living in the village on one side of the mountain call it East Mountain, and the people living in the village on the other side call it West Mountain. Even though the residents of both villages get together and argue endlessly about whether it's East Mountain or West Mountain, they never reach an agreement. Even though both sides are telling the truth, the problem can't be resolved. Historical records from one village say that the mountain is East Mountain because when you observe the direction of the sunrise, the sun rises over the mountain. The historical records of the other village show that the mountain is West

Mountain because the direction of the sunset is on their side of the mountain. It is obvious that the problem can't be solved by a majority vote, historical records, or actual observation.

However, if these people left their own village and observed the mountain from the other village's vantage point, they wouldn't argue anymore. They would find themselves saying, "Oh, it's not East Mountain," or "Oh, it's not West Mountain." Just like that, the argument would be settled. We are just like these villagers. We are caught up in our own experiences, beliefs, religions, thoughts, and our own ideologies. In Buddhism, this is the notion of self or self-attachment.

People arguing about whether a mountain is East Mountain or West Mountain are just like a wife and husband, Buddhists and Christians, North and South Koreans, or Koreans and Japanese arguing with each other. It's the ruling party versus the opposition party, progressives versus conservatives, employers versus workers, and one region of the country versus another. Those on each side claim they are right and give all kinds of evidence to prove their point. People on one side sit together, get worked up talking among themselves, and argue, "How could they insist East Mountain is West Mountain? They're nuts."

People fight with one other saying that whatever the opposition party says is always right and whatever the ruling party says is always wrong, that what Buddhists say is always right and what Christians say is always wrong, that what Koreans say is always right and what Japanese say is always wrong, and that what South Koreans say is always right and what North Koreans say is always wrong. People have different points of view. A wife's point of view is different from her husband's. An employer has a different perspective than his employee. A parent's viewpoint is different from her child's. So, in the eyes of the people on one side, the people on the other side are bound to look like lunatics who keep uttering the most ridiculous things.

But when you go to people on the opposite side, they insist it is the people on your side that are the ones saying crazy things. According to an old Korean proverb, "If you go to the kitchen, the daughter-in-law is right; and when you go to the living room, the mother-in-law is right." It's very natural for people born and raised in their respective villages to think that the mountain is East Mountain or West Mountain, depending on which side their village is located.

Koreans insist, "Dokdo* is our territory and so is Manchuria. And An Jung-geun** was a patriot." However, the Japanese claim, "Takeshima*** is our territory and An Jung-geun was a terrorist." Then, the Chinese maintain, "Manchuria is our territory." This argument can't be settled with a majority vote. If we try to rely on historical records, each country has records proving its claims. The arguing continues no matter what proof each side produces.

The solution here is that you need to leave your own village. Once outside, you can see that the mountain is neither East Mountain nor West Mountain. In other words, you can see that your claim is neither right nor wrong; it transcends right and wrong.

When a wife or husband comes to see me about marital conflict, I respond to their various questions in a way that goes outside the usual way of seeing things. Then, they think that I say these things because I'm not married, I don't

---

*   Dokdo consists of tiny islands contested by Korea and Japan, located in the East Sea.

**   A Korean independence fighter who assassinated the Prime Minister Ito Hirobumi of Japan in 1909.

***   Japanese name for Dokdo, the islands listed above.

have kids, and I haven't worked in an office. So, when I say things like "It's neither East Mountain nor West Mountain," the two people who were fighting until just a moment ago now become allies. Even though to them the mountain is definitely East Mountain, they can understand someone calling it West Mountain. However, saying it is neither East Mountain nor West Mountain seems totally absurd to them.

We need to break free from such confined ways of thinking. Otherwise, disputing what is true becomes meaningless. In such a situation, even if you prove yourself to be correct, the other person will keep thinking it's unfair. Let's say one village has a hundred people and the other has ten people. If the argument is settled by majority vote, the village with the ten residents will never accept it. They will keep it in their hearts, and when the opportunity arises, they will make their argument again. If they are forcefully suppressed, after some time, they will bounce back even stronger, like a coiled spring.

When a father who drinks every day and comes home at midnight scolds his child for coming home at 10 PM, the child will go to their room without saying a word and slam the door. Then, the parent will say, "What a brat. Slamming the door like that without saying anything…" But the child slamming the door is muttering under their breath, "How about you coming home early for a change?" If they think their mother or father will come into their room to berate them, they will quickly lock the door. What they mean to say is, "Mind your own business." If the child were to actually tell their father, "Dad, you should come home early," the father would say, "Why don't you mind your own business?" Since the child can't express their feelings directly, they are expressing them in a roundabout way.

When I call over my disciples to point out something they did wrong and to scold them, those who accept their mistake will do three bows as they leave, just like they did when entering the room. But those who don't accept their mistake will just leave without bowing. If that happens, I call them over again and explain, but sometimes they still can't understand what they did wrong. If they're caught up in their own way of thinking, even if I explain the issue ten times, they won't be able to hear or see the truth. They will only think, "How annoying. Why does he keep summoning me?" We all keep getting caught up in our own thoughts. I'm no different. We are all, more or less, the same.

How a Teacher and a Disciple
Became Sworn Enemies

The incident described below happened quite a long time ago. A young man came to see me while I was at a Buddhist practice center near Seoul. When he saw me, he prostrated himself three times and said, "I will become your disciple." So, I said to him, "I have no idea who you are. How do you know about me, and why do you want me to be your teacher?" He replied that he knew me well. He explained that he had spent a few months as a postulant in a number of temples under various eminent monks.

"I've been to several temples and none were like I had been led to believe. I lived with a number of so-called eminent monks, but I couldn't find anyone worthy enough to be a teacher. Then, I happened to read your book, Practical Buddhism and thought you would be a worthy teacher for me. I had to work very hard to find you, so please accept me as your disciple."

"Thank you for coming all this way, but I'm not yet qualified to be anyone's teacher. However, since you're here, why don't we live together as fellow practitioners?"

"My goodness, Sunim. What are you talking about? I came all the way here to find a teacher, not a fellow practitioner."

"Yes, I understand that. But I'm not qualified to be your teacher, so I'm suggesting that we live together as friends."

"That is such a humble thing to say, but if someone as great as you isn't qualified to be a teacher, who in the world would be?"

"It's not a simple matter, becoming a teacher and disciple."

"I know that."

"To attain nirvana, you must free yourself from the notion of self, the way you get caught up in your own thoughts. The teacher should be able to help the disciple awaken by breaking his notion of self. This is not easy. If things go wrong, the teacher and disciple can become sworn enemies. I neither have the ability to help others awaken nor do I want to become anyone's enemy. That's why I suggest you find another teacher or live with me as a friend."

Despite everything I said, he was fixated on the thought that I was qualified to be his teacher, and he stubbornly insisted on becoming my disciple. Anyone who had studied the Dharma would have seen their error right away, but he was unable to see that his insistence on becoming my disciple was not an aspiration but a manifestation of being caught up in his own thoughts. This young man was not showing respect to "Pomnyun Sunim," but instead was totally trapped in his own idea of who Pomnyun Sunim was.

Finally, I said, "If you sincerely wish me to be your teacher, I will do it. Will you be my disciple?"

He answered, "Yes!"

"From the moment you become my disciple, you can no longer insist on your ways. In all instances, you have to let go of your notions. If I tell you something, you have to answer with an unconditional 'yes.' Can you do that?"

"Yes, I'll do that! If you accept me as your disciple, I can certainly do that."

"Then, first of all, as my disciple, you need to pay proper respect to me by prostrating yourself three times. When you're finished, you and I will be disciple and teacher. To practice together, we need to respectively fulfill a teacher's duty and a disciple's duty. Our relationship will be nullified if I don't apply myself fully or if I neglect to do my duty as your teacher. It also becomes invalid if you don't respect me or fail to fulfill your duties as a disciple. If we are to have a teacher-disciple relationship, let's do it properly. I don't really want a disciple because if things go wrong we could become enemies. However, after you become my disciple, there is no turning back even if we end up becoming enemies."

"Good gracious! Sunim, how can we become sworn enemies? I really want to study under your guidance."

He prostrated himself three times with such respect that anyone could see he was sincere. Now that our teacher-disciple relationship had been established, I straightened my posture and called him by name, "So-and-so."

"Yes, Sunim."

"There is a monk in Mungyeong. Go to him and serve him as you would serve me and practice under him for three years."

"Pardon me? I promised to study under you as my teacher. I didn't promise to study under someone else."

"When you bowed three times to me, didn't that mean you now consider me your teacher?"

"Yes. I promised I would respect you as my teacher."

"What did I tell you about the duties of a disciple?"

"The duties of a disciple are to let go of one's own ways of thinking and accept the teacher's instructions without judgment."

"So-and-so."

"Yes, Sunim."

"There is a monk in Mungyeong. Go to him and practice under his guidance for three years."

"Sunim, why are you doing this? Didn't you just promise to take me as your disciple? Why are you already breaking your promise?"

Once again, I questioned him about the duties of a disciple. He answered that the disciple must trust the teacher and unconditionally follow the teacher's instructions. So, I told him to do as I asked, but he said he couldn't do that.

"Sunim, why are you really doing this? You just accepted me as your disciple so why do you keep changing your mind?"

"So-and-so, will you do what I say or not?"

"I will."

"Then, leave right now."

"No, Sunim. I will stay here."

"If you won't go to Mungyeong, then go home. You are no longer my disciple because you refuse to listen to me. You need to make up your mind. Will you go or not?"

"Do I have to?"

"Yes, you have to."

Reluctantly he agreed. "All right. I'll go."

"When you get there, you have to stay no matter what the monk says. No matter what, you are not to follow your own wishes or return here. Do you understand?"

"Yes, I'm sure I'll be fine there. I've lived in many different places, so it won't be difficult for me to live there. Don't worry."

He set out for Mungyeong but returned the next day. He said the monk ordered him to leave because he didn't need a disciple.

"What did I tell you? I told you to stay there no matter what. Why did you come back?"

"At first, I didn't budge even though he told me to leave. However, this morning, he presented me to the others during the morning assembly, and they decided not to accept me. When they make a decision during the assembly, it's final, so how could I stay? If I want to live in a temple, I need to follow the rules, don't I? That's why I came back."

I told him to return to Mungyeong immediately.

"I can't."

"Go now."

"No, I won't."

"If you don't go, our relationship as teacher and disciple will be over. If you want to continue to be my disciple, you have to return to Mungyeong."

"Sunim, do you really mean this?"

"Yes."

"Fine. You are not the only teacher in the world. I'll do fine on my own without you."

As a result, we became sworn enemies. I gave him several chances to fulfill my request as his teacher. I did this with affection but without being swayed by sympathy. However, that is just my point of view. The disciple would say that he strove to become my disciple despite the humiliation of being kicked out of the temple at Mungyeong, but in the end, I did not accept him as my disciple.

Holding the Bucket Upside Down

We say we understand what our spouse, parent, or child tells us. But do we really? When they say something to us, we tell them we get it. If they repeat it, we say, "I told you I got it," but in a slightly annoyed tone. If they continue repeating the same thing, we get angry and say, "What is your problem? I told you I got it!" This doesn't mean that we actually understand what the person was trying to tell us. It just means we don't want to hear it again.

There are also cases when we say, "I don't know." If they keep talking, we say, "I said I don't know." And if they still continue, we get angry and shout, "Look, I told you I don't know!" Here, also, we don't actually mean we don't know but just that we're tired of listening to them. If we really didn't know, we would ask for clarification. So, when we say "I got it," or "I don't know," it doesn't really mean that we understand or don't understand. It just means we don't want to hear it.

If you are caught up in the mentality of "I don't want to hear it" even the Buddha can't help you. When people stand in the rain holding a bucket to collect rainwater, the amount they collect will depend on how large or small the bucket is. There are also people who stand in the rain all day long and get soaking wet but fail to collect a single drop of rainwater. These are people who hold their buckets upside down. They're the ones who constantly say either "I got it," or "I don't know." They're the ones who are caught up in the mentality of "I don't want to hear it" and are imprisoned by their own thoughts. They mistakenly think that they're listening and seeing when, in reality, they are not. We're all locked into this pattern and need to break ourselves free.

The real problem is that we don't know we are imprisoned. Because of this, we wouldn't be able to recognize the Buddha even if he came into this world, and we wouldn't be able to hear what our teacher said even if we had a teacher. This is not the teacher's problem or the Buddha's problem. Unless we open our eyes, we cannot become free no matter how many Buddhas visit this world. Instead of blaming others, we need to focus on opening our own eyes. To do that, we need to really listen to what others say. But even then, we all listen based on our own thoughts. Only when we abandon our own ways and thoughts will we be able to really listen and see.

When I give a Dharma talk, many people in the audience nod their heads. If someone says, "Wow, you're right," does that mean they accept what I said? If someone says, "No, you're wrong," does that mean they reject what I said?

No, it doesn't. When someone nods their head, it means my opinion is the same as theirs. If someone shakes their head in disagreement, it means my opinion is different from theirs. They agree with me not because my Dharma talk is right but because it coincides with their own thoughts. It means, "He thinks like me. He makes sense." If they shake their heads, it means, "Listen to him. His opinion is different from mine. His thinking is flawed."

Knowing this, I'm not fooled when you either agree or

disagree with me. I'm not taken in by your praise or your criticism. If I let it fool me, that will be my loss. If praises make me feel buoyant, like I can fly, I'll tumble to the ground and break my back when the bubble bursts. If I'm fooled and tormented by criticism and can't sleep, that is also my loss. Everyone thinks in their own way. We have to learn to break free from this. That is practice.

When 100 people sleep in the same room, they all have different dreams. Even when we sleep right next to someone, our dreams are different. We all live in totally different worlds. Our own thoughts are like that dream. When we're caught up in our individual thoughts, each of us is living in a totally different world. We may occupy the same space, but we live in completely different dimensions and worlds. It's the same for married couples. Even though they live together, they can feel lonely, stifled, and unhappy when they don't understand each other. We interact closely with others and even though we are surrounded by people, we still feel alone. That's because we are trapped inside our own thoughts. We need to break away from our thoughts to become free and see the world as it is.

Saying "Yes"
When You Really Don't Want To

No one should criticize the disciple I mentioned earlier. I am like that myself. My own teacher would think that young man and I are quite similar. Even when my teacher tells me how to do something a hundred times, I don't listen and just do it my way. It would be better if we could become awakened in moments like these, but, at the very least, we need to recognize that this is how we are. We need to be aware that even when we make up our minds to say "yes" no matter what, we actually don't. If we know this about ourselves, then we won't get angry and upset when others don't listen to us because this is how ordinary people are.

People say things like, "I made that investment, trusting the information so-and-so gave me, but I was swindled." But that isn't true. Each of us makes judgments and decisions and acts accordingly every minute of the day. When something suits us, we nod our heads, and when something doesn't suit us, we shake our heads.

To attain enlightenment, you must flip your thoughts upside down and say "yes" when you're inclined to say "no." Saying "yes" when that would've been your natural response has no merit. When you're thinking, "No way, that's not right," in that instant, those who practice need to flip their thoughts 180 degrees and just say "yes." But even if you're given a thousand opportunities, it's very difficult to do it even once.

From now on, practice saying "yes." Say "yes" when your spouse, parent, or child says something that makes you think, "I don't know about other things, but that can't be right." Just try saying "yes." You may think the sky will fall and the world will come to an end if you say "yes." However, when nothing happens, your eyes will be opened. There's a phrase about this in Seon Buddhism: "To take one more step forward from the edge of a cliff 100 meters high." When you think, "There's absolutely no way I can take one more step; I'll fall to my death if I do," or "This is as far as I'll go," that's when you need to take that additional step. This is important. Give it a try. Tackle it head-on with the attitude of, "How bad can it be? Let me try it even if it kills me." Saying "yes" only after carefully weighing the options and deciding it's worth a shot won't take you far.

Practice should be like this. For worldly matters, you should think about the different ways to accomplish something and discuss those choices with others. But when it comes to practice that will lead you to enlightenment, you must do away with such shrewdness. There is no need to discuss what practice is or who does or doesn't practice well. The practice to attain enlightenment cannot be given or taken. Nor is practice blindly following orders like a soldier in the military.

Why do they say we have to let ourselves go to become our own master? Why can't we be our own master while we hold onto ourselves? The Dharma should not be viewed as a compilation of concepts or a matter of ability. Of course, this doesn't mean that we don't need concepts or abilities either. But you can't reach nirvana and liberation, the world of true freedom, through these things.

We must transcend the contradictions that exist in a conceptual world. Seon riddles expose such contradictions. When the teacher asks a question, the disciple will be beaten 30 times with a wooden staff if they open their mouth, but they will also be beaten 30 times if they stay silent. They received a question, so they have to answer it. But if they open their mouth, they'll be hit 30 times, so this is a contradiction.

This is sometimes explained using the metaphor of asking a question to a person hanging on for dear life off a cliff by barely holding onto a branch with his mouth. If they open their mouths to answer the question, they will fall and die. However, if they don't answer the question, they can't attain enlightenment. The lesson here is that you need to transcend death, but this death isn't about physical death.

To break free from the thoughts you're caught up in, you must take a step over the cliff edge. The idea is "to take one more step forward from the edge of a cliff 100 meters high" and enter a new world. To be free, you must walk through the gate that blocks you. Then, even though your mind wavers from moment to moment due to external obstacles, since you are aware of it, you can quickly return to a calm state of mind. In that sense, we use the expression, "transcending the fear of life and death." This is because life and death are also mental constructs we are holding onto.

PART 03

REFLECT UPON YOURSELF

We need to acknowledge that, as human beings, we tend to get caught up in the idea of "self," and, thus, we need to constantly examine ourselves. Even though we can't break away from our own viewpoint, at the very least, we shouldn't insist on it. Then, even though our eyes are not open, we won't scream, "It's dark. Turn on the light."

We need to be able to distinguish why it's dark. Is it because there is no light or because our eyes are closed? If it's still dark when others say the lights are on, we should be able to look at ourselves to see if our eyes are closed rather than getting angry or screaming for someone to turn on the lights. Only then can we proceed to the next step – opening our eyes.

The Story of Lady Bodeok

This story takes place at a small Budddhist temple called Bodeokam, located in the inner valley of Mt. Geumgang.* Bodeokam Temple was built off a sheer rock cliff, on a wooden platform secured by iron chains and bronze pillars driven into the cliff. Located behind the temple is a small cave. Bodeokam has ties to the Venerable Bodeok Hwasang,** the founder of the Yeolban School of Buddhism, the most prominent among the five doctrinal schools and

---

* Mt. Geumgang is a mountain located in North Korea renowned for its scenic beauty. It is also known as a mountain that carries the spirit of the Korean people.

** Hwasang is a Korean term of respect for Buddhist monks.

the nine schools of Seon Buddhism that existed during the Silla Dynasty (57 BC to 935 AD). Bodeok Hwasang was born in Goguryeo. But when Buddhism was oppressed during the last years of the Gogureo Dynasty, he fled south to the neighboring kingdom of Baekje. This is a story about Hoejeong Sunim, the successor of Bodeok Hwasang, who was born during the mid-Goryeo period, roughly 500 years after Bodeok Hwasang.

Hoejeong Sunim became a monk at an early age and practiced diligently at Songnaam Temple, a branch of the Janganasa Temple in Mt. Geumgang, but he never managed to attain enlightenment. He believed in Bodhisattva Avalokiteshvara, but he had yet to meet the embodiment of the bodhisattva. So, he began a thousand-day prayer and prayed with devotion, with the hope that she would appear to him.

There are several different ways of praying to Avalokite-

The Silla Dynasty was one of the ancient Three Kingdoms of Korea. The other two were Goguryeo and Baekje.

Goguryeo was one of the Three Kingdoms of Korea, located in the northern and central part of the Korean peninsula (37 BC-668 AD).

A bodhisattva of compassion and mercy known as Gwaneum or Gwanseeum Bosal in Korean.

shvara. You can chant the name of Avalokiteshvara, the sutra of Great Dharani, or "Om Mani Padme Hum." Hoejeong Sunim decided to chant the Great Dharani Sutra 300,000 times during the one thousand days. This meant he would have to chant the sutra 300 times each day, which would take about 15 hours. So, he rose very early each morning and chanted nonstop, only pausing for meals and sleep. He chanted the sutra with complete focus and dedication. As the last day of the thousand-day prayer was fast approaching, a noble lady in a white robe appeared to him while he was chanting. He couldn't tell if she was real or a dream.

She said, "Because you have prayed with such sincerity, I will tell you how to meet the embodiment of Bodhisattva Avalokiteshvara. If you go to the valley of Seoraegok, you will find an old man by the name of Molgol-ong, and also another old man called Haemyeongbang, who lives with his daughter. If you go there, you will be able to see the embodiment of Avalokiteshvara."

When Hoejeong Sunim returned to his senses, the lady was gone, and he was left to wonder whether he had dozed

---

Molgol-ong means a "very shabby-looking old man."

Haemyeongbang means the "spirit of elucidation."

off while chanting. But the scene remained so vivid that he immediately slung his knapsack on his back and set out to find the place the lady spoke about. Believing that his thousand-day prayer had finally been answered, he was ecstatic that he would finally get to meet Avalokiteshvara. However, no one he met on his travels seemed to know where Seoraegok was located. One man discouraged him, saying that the valley was hidden deep in the mountains and that he would find nothing to eat there. When Hoejeong assured the man there was no need to worry, he finally told him the way to Seoraegok. The man also explained how no one ever went there, but if he followed the valley and climbed for miles, he would eventually arrive at Seoraegok.

Hoejeong Sunim walked all day, crossing streams, climbing up the mountain, and traveling down the valley walls until, just as the sun was setting, he discovered a small thatched-roof hut. As he drew near, he noticed a very shabby-looking old man. With his filthy clothes, unwashed hair, and runny nose, he clearly looked like a "very shabby-looking old man." When Hoejeong asked who the man was, the man replied that indeed he was Molgol-ong. Heojeong explained why he had come and asked him to tell him how to find Haemyeongbang.

Since it was growing dark, the man invited the young monk to stay for the night. When Molgol-ong offered Hoejeong some acorn jelly to eat, the monk hesitated because the old man's hands were so dirty, but he was too hungry to refuse the meal. The following morning, the man told him how to find Haemyeongbang and added, "I'm not sure you can do it, but bear in mind that Haemyeongbang has a very bad temper. Good luck." The monk replied, "Don't worry. I came here willing to risk my life!"

He headed out, following the valley, hiking over a hill into the next valley as the old man had instructed. During the journey, he found himself captivated by the beauty of his surroundings. Finally, in the distance, he spotted a small hut perched on top of a cliff. Expecting another old man to answer his knock, he was startled when a beautiful young woman answered the door. He hadn't laid eyes on any women since becoming a monk, and what were the chances of meeting such a beautiful young woman in such an isolated place, deep in the mountains? Trying to calm down his racing pulse, he told her he was searching for an old man called Haemyeongbang, and she told him that he had come to the right place. She said that Haemyeongbang was her father, and she asked him to wait a while since he was off gathering wood.

Seeing how thirsty he was after his long walk, the young woman offered him a gourd filled with water before asking why he wished to speak with her father. He quickly explained the reason he'd come, and she invited him inside to wait. It was the custom back then for males and females over the age of seven to not be together in the same room unchaperoned. On top of that, he was a monk, so Hoejeong Sunim hesitated entering the house occupied only by a young woman. However, she kept asking him to step inside the hut, so he relented.

While they talked, she gave him a piece of advice. She said that her father had a hot temper and was easily angered, and he would have to be patient with the older man if he wanted to meet the embodiment of Avalokiteshvara. She told him to stay put and not run away, regardless of the hardships he was subjected to. Suddenly, he heard something hit the ground outside with a thud. When the monk stepped outside, he saw an old man removing a wooden carrier full of wood from his back. The moment the old man caught sight of the monk, he started to shout, "Who the hell are you to enter a house with an unchaperoned girl inside and try to seduce her? You thief!"

Without giving Hoejeong Sunim a chance to explain, the old man began hitting his head with a stick. The more the monk tried to explain, the harder the old man beat him. But he couldn't turn away. He begged the old man to show him the way to meet the embodiment of Avalokiteshvara and explained that he had done his thousand-day prayer and had come all this way for that reason. But this only seemed to make the old man even angrier.

"A paltry thousand-day prayer has not earned you the right to see the Bodhisattva Avalokiteshvara. Even a ten-thousand-day prayer wouldn't be enough."

"Please just let me stay. I'll do whatever you tell me to do. Please don't send me away."

The old man asked, "Really? You'll do whatever I tell you to do?"

"Yes, yes. Whatever you tell me to do, I'll do my best."

"Then, get up."

The old man ushered the young man inside as though nothing had happened. All of a sudden, he ordered the monk to marry his daughter. Hoejeong Sunim was dumbfounded. He had entered the monastery at an early age and had already practiced as a monk for 20 years with the sole aspiration of seeing the embodiment of Avalokiteshvara. So, how could he suddenly accept renouncing his vows as a monk and becoming a layman?

"Goodness, sir. I will do anything but that."

"You scoundrel! You just promised that you would do your damnedest to do whatever I told you to do. How can you say you can't marry my daughter? Is that more difficult than dying? Isn't she pretty enough for you?"

The old man began hitting him again. The monk begged the old man to spare him, saying how could he get married now after practicing as a monk for 20 years. But the old man just called him a liar. Just then, the young woman caught his eye and signaled that he should consent to her father's request. The monk himself was worried that if he didn't agree, the old man would beat him to death or throw him out and that he would never get to see the embodiment of Avalokiteshvara. So, he conceded reluctantly. "All right. I'll marry her."

As soon as the monk said that, the old man began arranging

the wedding ceremony as if nothing out of the ordinary had just happened. He told the monk to spread out a straw mat and to fill a bowl with water and place it in the middle of the mat. He instructed Hoejeong Sunim and his daughter to face each other and bow to each another. Then, the old man ended the wedding ceremony by declaring, "You two are now married," and told them to go into the next room and go to sleep. As the monk entered the room, he felt like he was waking from a dream. He asked the young woman her name, and she told him that her father named her Bodeok, so people called her Lady Bodeok.

He still couldn't believe what had just happened; his practice of 20 years had vanished in the blink of an eye. He sighed, feeling as though a goblin had cast a magic spell on him. Then, he heard Lady Bodeok's sweet voice. "There's no use crying over spilled milk, is there? Try to relax and go to sleep."

She was right. Today, people get divorced even if they have children. However, back then, even if the parents of two families only verbally promised to betrothe their children, the couple got married, no matter what. "Oh well!" he thought. "What will be will be." He stopped resisting and lay down next to his wife to sleep.

Earlier that day, breaking his vow of celibacy had felt unbearable, but now, lying next to his wife, thinking that it was too late to turn things around, he started to feel something change in his heart. Cautiously, he tried to take his wife's hands, but she kept pulling them away. After several attempts, he became aroused and held her hands so tightly she couldn't pull away. She resisted when he tried to touch her breasts, so he embraced her. Moving his hands down to her navel and then lower, he became even more aroused. His wife was now powerless to stop him. When his hand reached her groin, he discovered her sexual organs were underdeveloped. He jerked his hand away and sat up. That's when he realized her father had forced him to marry her because she was not a complete woman. He thought that was why the old man had beaten and terrorized him from the moment he saw him.

His head was spinning. Against his will, he had broken his vow of celibacy, and now he was being denied one of the basic pleasures of married life. Talk about adding insult to injury. Disappointed and angry, he let out a long heavy sigh.

His wife sat up and quietly said, "Husband, isn't it better

this way? Weren't you fighting so hard not to break your vow just a short while ago?" Even though her words made sense, he had trouble accepting the situation. But her beauty and sweet voice helped him to gradually calm down. The truth was, what could he do? He decided to give up both his practice and any hope of having a real marriage and concentrate his efforts on meeting the embodiment of Avalokiteshvara.

The next day, the old man put him to work doing hard physical labor. Early in the morning, he would climb the mountain and gather wood, which he carried to a distant market to trade for food. He was no longer a monk, he was married but didn't really have a wife, and now he felt like an unpaid farmhand. Eventually, he lost sight of why he'd come there in the first place and became increasingly more disgruntled. Whenever he asked the old man when he would be able to meet Avalokiteshvara, the old man would beat him with a stick, yelling that he'd only been working for a few days when a ten-thousand-day prayer wouldn't be sufficient.

At first, he endured his new life. He thought he would wait a year before leaving. At the end of the first year, he again asked about meeting Avalokiteshvara. The old man said even someone who had done a ten-thousand-day prayer wasn't guaranteed to meet her, so he was asking too much only after three years of prayer and one year of work. Because his wife was very kind to him, he decided to wait one more year. After enduring that year, he asked the old man again but only got another beating. This made him so furious he decided to leave, but, once again, his wife soothed his anger. He thought, "I spent three years praying, didn't I? There's no reason I can't work for three years. I'm already ruined, so I'll stay for just one more year." He gritted his teeth and endured one more year.

This is how three years passed. And still, he hadn't had the opportunity to meet the embodiment of Avalokiteshvara. He could no longer bear it and decided to leave, no matter how gently his wife might try to dissuade him and calm him down.

He declared, "I can't stand it. I'll be going now." Previously, when he'd said that, the old man had scolded and beaten him, but this time, the old man just nonchalantly told him to go. Also, his wife, who had taken such good care of him, simply said goodbye and wished him well. He should have felt relieved that she wasn't trying to keep him there, but instead, he wondered how she could let him go so easily. He felt disappointed, feeling as if the past three years of sleeping under the same covers had meant nothing to her. He kept glancing back over his shoulder as he began hiking down the mountain, but neither the old man nor Bodeok glanced his way.

Retracing his steps, he met Molgol-ong, the shabby old man, again. Molgol-ong asked if he'd met Avalokiteshvara. Hoejeong Sunim complained that he had been beaten and enslaved as an unpaid farmhand, and had even broken his vow of celibacy, but still hadn't met the embodiment of Avalokiteshvara. Grabbing a stick, Molgol-ong hit him hard on the head. "You idiot! You slept under the same blanket with Bodhisattva Avalokiteshvara for three years, and you didn't recognize her?"

Imagine how stunned the monk was. He asked Molgol-ong who Haemyeongbang was and was told he was Samantabhadra.*

"Then, who are you?"

---

* Bodhisattva Samantabhadra is a bodhisattva associated with practice and meditation.

"I am Manjusri."[*] The words had barely registered before he disappeared. Hoejeong Sunim hurried back to the place where he had lived with his wife, but everything was gone. When he returned to where Molgol-ong's house had been, it, too, was gone.

Filled with regret, he made his way back to Songnaam Temple. He hadn't recognized Avalokiteshvara even though he'd lived with her for three years. Why? Because he'd been caught up in his own thoughts. So, he offered a prayer of repentance. "I will let go now of the delusion that I will meet the embodiment of Avalokiteshvara. I've been blind and foolish."

He again prayed with all his heart for three years, and the noble lady once more appeared in a dream. She scolded him, "How foolish you are to have lived with Avalokiteshvara for three years and not recognize her." There was nothing he could say. The lady continued to rebuke him for a while before saying, "Since you have sincerely repented, go back to that place." Then, she disappeared.

His mind was no longer the same. By now, he'd believe it

---

[*] Bodhisattva Manjusri is a bodhisattva associated with wisdom.

A Taste of Enlightenment

if someone told him a block of wood was Avalokiteshvara.

He returned to the place where the house had stood and reminisced about the time he had spent there. When he gazed down the mountainside, he saw his wife washing clothes by a stream. Elated to see her, he ran toward her, calling her name. When he got to the spot, there was no trace of her, but he saw a very beautiful bird fly away. This bird was called Gwaneum-jo, the bird of Avalokiteshvara. The monk followed the bird as it flew up the valley until it, too, suddenly disappeared. As he stood there not knowing what to do next, he looked down in the puddle by his feet, and there, he saw the reflection of his wife. When he raised his head, he saw her standing at the entrance of a cave, high up on the steep cliff.

Arduously, he climbed up the cliff holding on to the kudzu vines. Lady Bodeok greeted him joyfully. She told him that he was the reincarnation of Bodeok Hwasang, who had lived 500 years earlier, and that this was the spot where Bodeok Hwasang had practiced, praying to Bodhisattva Avalokiteshvara. "I am always in this cave," she told him, "and if someone comes, I appear in a form that is in accordance with that person's karmic affinity. You need to continue practicing diligently, with all your heart."

Then, Avalokiteshvara once again vanished. When the monk returned to his senses, he looked around the cave and saw a statue of Avalokiteshvara, whose features were identical to those of his wife of three years. He also saw incense burners, candle holders, and various Buddhist sutras such as the *Mahayana Mahaparinirvana Sutra*, *Lotus Sutra*, and *Diamond Sutra*. There was also a record of how Bodeok Hwasang had practiced there, praying to Bodhisattva Avalokiteshvara.

Heojeong Sunim built a small temple above the Bodeok Cave, where he did as Lady Bodeok had requested and practiced diligently with valor and devotion. Eventually, he attained enlightenment. He is known to have played a big role in spreading the faith about Bodhisattva Avalokiteshvara during the Goryeo period, building Bomunsa Temple and Jeongsusa Temple in Ganghwa Province. This is the story of Lady Bodeok.

Let's examine this story more closely. Hoejeong Sunim prayed devotedly for three years with the sole purpose of meeting Avalokiteshvara. He promised the old man, Haemyeongbang, that he would do anything he told him to do, even at the risk of dying, if only he would let him stay. But when the old man told him to marry his daughter, Hoejeong Sunim said he would do anything but that.

The monk was caught up in his own thoughts. When people think an act is morally right, they will do it even though their lives are threatened. However, if they think it is wrong, they will refuse to do it even if it is the Buddha's words. This is being attached to the notion of self or insisting on one's thoughts. When, in an instant, your mind gets caught up in a thought, you must break away from it. To do this, you need to be mindful enough to notice the changes that occurred in your mind. We say that we will let go of our own thoughts, but every single time, we simply continue stubbornly holding onto them. Sometimes, we even get caught up in the idea of letting go of our notion of self. In order to let go, we need to acknowledge and be aware that we are stubbornly holding onto our thoughts, but that is something we can rarely do.

Breaking the notion of self is saying "yes" when someone says something you don't agree with. But we find this almost impossible to do and, thus, continue to live according to our own karma. Therefore, no matter how many times the

Buddha comes to this world, we cannot recognize him. No matter how great a teacher is, we fail to recognize them. It's like the person who closes their eyes and then blames the world for the darkness. No matter how many lights are turned on, the world remains dark if you keep your eyes closed. Rather than turning on the lights, you need to open your eyes. Opening your eyes and waking from your dream is awakening. You have to break away from being caught up in your own thoughts. Only when you free yourself from the notion of self, can you see the Buddha.

Hoejeong Sunim had several opportunities to become enlightened. The first was when he said he would do anything to remain with Haemyeongbang except marrying his daughter. This occurred just moments after he'd promised to do anything if he could only meet the embodiment of Avalokiteshvara. He continued to be caught up in his own way of thinking. That's why he thought the old man was making absurd requests. He couldn't see the contradiction in his own actions.

What would have happened if he'd realized he was trapped in his own thoughts and let them go? He would have immediately attained enlightenment, as quickly as opening one's eyes, but he kept missing his chance. Instead, after insisting he couldn't break his vow of celibacy, once he was married, he had no trouble breaking it. Then, when he discovered his wife had underdeveloped sexual organs, he felt disappointed that he could not consummate the marriage because he'd become attached to the thought of being married.

Marrying Haemyeongbang's daughter shouldn't have been such a difficult thing to accept since he had already agreed to do anything the old man told him to do as long as he was allowed to stay. When the old man demanded he marry his daughter, the monk should have said, "Wow, this is great! I get to stay and even get married." Instead, he insisted that he could do anything but get married.

Next, he should have been relieved and happy to discover his wife had underdeveloped sexual organs because it allowed him to keep his vow of celibacy. This would have allowed him to remain there, get married, and keep his vow, all at the same time. It was like killing two birds with one stone. But Hoejeong Sunim believed that he'd lost everything. He believed he had broken his vow, only to find out he couldn't have a normal married life and children. That is what happens when we get caught up in our thoughts.

If a raft is stuck against the bank on one side of a river, it won't move. If you push it hard and send it to the opposite side, it will then get stuck on the other side. This is going back and forth between two extremes. Likewise, our thoughts keep leaning to one extreme or the other.

There are times when people regret getting married and think about getting a divorce, right? But, let's say, if the husband has an affair, the wife will be unhappy. She will track down the other woman and fight tooth and nail to get her husband back. Then, when her husband returns home, she will say, "How could you cheat on me?" and kick him out. If the husband actually leaves, she will chase after him and try to bring him back. We are constantly acting in such contradictory ways, but at the time, we don't see it. To see our contradictions, we have to look inside ourselves, but, instead, we look externally, so we fail to see them.

In the End, It's Your Decision

A woman asked me for advice. She said her husband made her life very difficult. I told her there was no reason for her to live with someone like that and that she should divorce him. She replied that divorce was impossible because of her children.

"Let your husband raise them," I told her.

"They're too young to be raised by him."

"Then, raise them yourself."

She explained that it would be difficult enough to live on her own without being responsible for raising her children. She said she was already emotionally detached from her husband, but she was worried about the children, making the divorce complicated. However, throughout the conversation, it was apparent to me that she wanted to continue living with her husband rather than get a divorce. She went on and on about why it was impossible to maintain her marriage. She said that her husband had a bad temper, was unfaithful, drank too much, and so on. Had I advised her that she should try saving the marriage while sympathizing with her, I think she would have gladly taken my advice while acting reluctant on the surface. Instead, I told her to divorce him. That wasn't what she wanted to hear because she then started to list all the reasons why she couldn't get a divorce, including using her children as an excuse.

She returned several years later and said she was now determined to get a divorce. "When I asked for your advice last time, I really felt I couldn't leave my husband because of my children. Since then, I have listened to your Dharma talks and practiced, which helped me maintain my marriage. But I don't think I can anymore, for the sake of my children's education. I've had enough of him getting drunk and cursing and beating me. What would my children learn from that?"

I took this to mean that she was leaning toward the argument that she could no longer live with her husband. Most people who come to see me have already made up their minds on the issue they seek advice on, so only a few people take my advice. Once I understood this, counseling them became very easy. Since they had already made up their minds, all I had to do was agree with their decisions. If they seemed disappointed that I agreed with them, it means they're leaning toward the other option they held in their heart.

Let's say a woman insists she needs to get a divorce, and I tell her to go ahead and get the divorce. If she thanks me and takes my advice immediately, it means that she had almost made up her mind before she came to see me. In that case, disagreeing with her would only be a waste of time. On the other hand, if she replies that she can't get a divorce because of her children, it means she has more reasons to stay married than to get divorced. When she is very angry at her husband, she gets caught up in the idea that she wants a divorce. But when somebody advises her to do so, she starts to remember the benefits of staying in the marriage and can't let go of them.

I can discover where a person stands by pressing one side of the scale and then the other. For most people, the ratio between two choices is 45% vs. 55% or 48% vs. 52% or even 49% vs. 51%. Differences that small makes it harder for people to come to a decision. When the difference is much greater, such as 20% vs. 80%, they don't seek advice. They simply make their decision without any hesitation. People come to me when the difference is much smaller. But that doesn't make the counseling difficult or challenging. It's actually very easy because the decision doesn't make much of a difference one way or the other. Whatever the decision, the benefits or losses will be similar, and they'll have a lingering attachment to the option they did not choose. Even if I make a decision for them, they'll go to another person to ask the same question. In the end, they won't follow my advice.

So, counseling is very easy for me. In most cases, the questioner will end up doing whatever they want. The main reason they seek my advice is that they don't want to be solely responsible for their choice. Then, if things don't turn out well, they can blame me. It's a matter of psychological comfort. They feel more comfortable with their decision if I am on their side. When the scale is swaying, even if I barely press one side, it will tilt to that side. But if one side is definitely heavier, it won't tilt to the other side no

A Taste of Enlightenment

matter how much pressure I place on it. This is why I don't interfere in other people's lives. Experience has led me to this conclusion.

When people say their lives got better after listening to my Dharma talks, any kind of awakening that they experienced was due to their own strength or merit; it's not because of what I told them. I just assisted them a little when they were almost at the point of awakening. If they were nowhere close, they wouldn't have been awakened no matter how hard I tried to help them. How would I be able to help awaken anyone who was so caught up in their own thoughts that they don't recognize what is happening in their own lives? Remember Hoejeong Sunim, who was so caught up in his own thoughts that he didn't recognize Bodhisattva Avalokiteshvara even after living with her for three years.

Husband Buddha,
Wife Buddha

The husband, wife, parent, or child who lives with you could be the embodiment of Avalokiteshvara. Even if your husband drinks and gives you a hard time, how can you be sure that he is not Avalokiteshvara? It's possible you haven't recognized Avalokiteshvara because you are distracted by external circumstances even when she manifests herself in countless forms, trying to help you awaken.

Once you are awakened, you will be able to see that clearly. You complain about your husband having an affair or your child not doing well in school and getting into trouble. But if your husband or child had not given you that much trouble, you would never have come and listened to Dharma talks or be doing 108 bows of chamhoe° every morning. When you are well off, you believe it's because of your own luck, and you spend your time enjoying your prosperity. It's only because you had worries and concerns that you went to temples, churches, or counselors until you finally settled at Jungto Society. Most of the people who come here are headstrong. They only come here after they've already tried everything else to fix their problems without any success. They're not likely to listen to anyone else unless there is no other choice.

Once you are awakened, you know that the problem isn't your husband's or your children's but yours. Also, you will know that you wouldn't have considered learning the Dharma and practicing if it weren't for your husband or children giving you such a hard time. You'll start to see that, by causing you trouble, your children were sacrificing themselves to lead you to this path. Similarly, you'll see that your husband went to great lengths, even drinking and becoming violent, to lead you to your awakening.

° Self-reflecting on one's mistakes and vowing never to make the same mistake again.

If you consider
someone close to you,
like a husband or a parent,
as your coach,
your practice will
progress rapidly.

At this point, you'll naturally feel grateful and begin to treat them better. This is the moment when your husband or your child becomes the embodiment of a bodhisattva. Once your eyes are open, your husband is Avalokiteshvara, Manjushri, or Samantabhadra. If your husband still gives you headaches, it means that your eyes are not open yet.

In the field of sports, a coach follows his trainees around and gives detailed instructions on how to move their head, hands, or other body parts. This is to improve the athlete's performance. Just like the coach, your spouse may be coaching you on how to practice and maintain mindfulness. If you show even a little anger, your spouse will let you know that is the wrong way for a practitioner to behave. Your spouse will often say, "You should treat me as you treat Pomnyun Sunim."

A coach might not be the best player, but they know their sport better than anyone else. No matter how famous a coach may be, they don't play the sport better than their players. If they did, they would have been the players. But coaches understand the sport like no one else does. Family members are like coaches. When you say something, they immediately question whether your words are in accordance with my Dharma talks. And they never fail to notice the moment you get caught up in your thoughts. For you, they are better coaches than I am.

If you would like to know whether you have made any progress in your practice, the quickest and easiest way is to ask your family. A wife can ask her husband. A husband can ask his wife. A parent can ask their child, and the child can ask their parent. Some people come to me to ask how much progress they have made. That is a difficult thing for me to know, so I say, "Let me ask your spouse."

If you consider someone close to you, such as a partner or a parent, as your coach, your practice will progress rapidly. You will have a better environment for practice than an ordained monk because every minute of the day you will have a coach who guides you in your every move.

Go to Another Temple

When I was a Dharma teacher at a temple in Gyeongju, I gave Dharma talks for children and students of different ages, working hard to spread the Buddha's teachings. One day, while I was performing the morning chanting in the Buddha Hall, someone knocked so loudly it sounded like a steel rod hitting the door. Even though I continued to strike the moktak* to accompany the chanting, I kept thinking, "Who the hell is that? They're going to break down the door." The noise filled my mind until I couldn't stand it

---

* A simple hollow wooden percussion instrument used during Buddhist ceremonies and daily chanting.

any longer, so I put the moktak down. I was very angry but managed to calm myself. I threw open the door and found a disabled veteran standing in the doorway. He had a hook where one of his arms should have been. The hook was why he'd made such a racket when he knocked. As soon as I saw him, I thought he'd come to beg and asked him to wait until I finished the morning chanting. I turned around to continue the chanting only to have him bang on the door again. I wondered why he couldn't show some patience if he came here to beg. I put down the moktak, opened the door, and began to scold him, "I told you to wait. As you can see, I am very busy."

"You're not the only one who is busy. I'm busy, too."

"No matter how busy you think you are, you need to wait until I can go to the living quarters to get rice or money to give you. I can't do that in the middle of the morning chanting, so please wait."

"When did I ask you for money?"

Even though I hadn't given him a chance to say a word, I'd assumed he had come to beg. I was still preoccupied with the desire to finish the chanting, but his words surprised me. So, I asked him why he was here if it wasn't to beg.

A Taste of Enlightenment

"I came here to become a monk." His words angered me. This was the early 1980s, and the memory of the October 27 crackdown on Buddhist monks by the Chun Doo-hwan administration* was still fresh in my mind. Because of this experience, I assumed he viewed monks with disdain and that he believed anyone who wanted to be a monk would be accepted.

"Oh, really" I said, "But this is a place where children are educated, not a place where you can study to become a monk." Waving my hand, I told him, "You need to go to the temple on the mountain over there." He replied, "I've already been to all those places, but none would accept me. Every time, they told me to go to another temple."

I asked him why he wanted to become a monk. He answered that he felt frustrated. I again suggested he go to another temple as ours was not a place where monks were trained. He replied that he'd already been to several other temples with no success. Then, someone told him about our temple and gave him a flyer. He showed it to me. It was an

---

* Former President Chun Doo-hwan ordered a brutal crackdown on Buddhist monks on October 27, 1980 to remove the administrative head of the Korean Buddhist Jogye Order, who the Chun administration considered a dissident.

advertisement I'd handed out on the street a few days earlier to spread the Buddha's teachings. On the top, in bold letters, it said, "Anybody who feels frustrated is welcome. Here is a wonderful refuge the Buddha has prepared for you." I had made two thousand copies and handed them out to people on the street.

"I feel frustrated," he repeated, beating his chest. If this had happened today, I would have been able to say something to him, but at the time, I was teaching Buddhism from books. I had no idea what to say to someone who was feeling frustrated. I could explain the Four Noble Truths, the Law of Dependent Origination, and the Noble Eightfold Path without a hitch, but I had no idea what to say to that man. All I could do was sit down and listen to the reasons why he was feeling so frustrated. In the mid-1960s, he volunteered to fight in the Vietnam War as a way to earn money even though his family opposed his decision. He lost an arm and a leg in the war, returning home as a disabled veteran. He couldn't get a job, so he stayed home while his wife supported him. The marriage was unhappy. They fought a lot, and eventually, he tried to kill himself but failed. He thought that by becoming a monk, he could renounce the world. However, every temple he had visited rejected him, giving one excuse or another. I imagine if he had been younger and more able-bodied, they would have accepted him.

Those temples were not the only ones that had rejected him; I also rejected him. When I look back, I realize that I tried to chase him away by giving him a little bit of money. When that didn't work, I tried to discourage him by saying the temple specialized in children's education. At the time, in my Dharma talks, I would always say we needed to break away from the established practice of Buddhism that is detached from worldly concerns and that we needed to practice Buddhism in our daily life and take care of the people who are suffering. That was the main message I delivered in my Dharma talks every single day. But, as soon as a person in pain showed up at my door, I did everything I could to get rid of him. I had no idea I had such a contradiction inside me. I was utterly shocked when the man revealed he'd come to see me because of the words that I had put on the flyer. The minute I saw the flyer, my mind went blank. I realized at that moment that I was a hypocrite and that I had been fooling not only other people but also myself.

After he left, I was too shocked to make sense of what I had learned about myself. I was shocked just as you would be when you find out that your spouse, parent, or child has just died, or that you have lost all of your life savings. I had left my family and everything I owned to live according to the Buddha's teachings, but I realized that I had been puffed up with pride as if I were different from all the other people in the world. My mind went blank, and my world collapsed all at once like I had lost my parents, siblings, children, and all of my life savings at the same time. Even though my eyes were open, it felt like I was blind. Whatever I had been saying until then rang hollow.

I thought to myself, "I can't go out into the world in this state. I shouldn't give Dharma talks or teach Buddhism until I attain enlightenment. I've been such a hypocrite, telling people I could liberate them when I couldn't even liberate myself."

I decided to travel to a remote mountain and stay there. I went to Chilbulam Temple where I had often visited to pray after I became a Buddhist. When I got there, I prostrated myself in front of the Buddha statue for days, not knowing if it was day or night, hot or cold.

I realized something there. If I had not handed out the flyers, I wouldn't have met the disabled veteran and seen myself for who I truly was. Even though I had been under the delusion that I was better than others, I got to see myself clearly because of my efforts to spread the Buddha's teachings. I arrived at the conclusion that everything that happened has contributed to my practice.

There was one more thing I realized. Until then, I had believed that abbots of large temples were obsessed with money and only cared about themselves. However, I could see there was no difference between them and me, in the sense that we were all caught up in our own thoughts. I believed that I was doing the right thing by spreading the Buddha's teachings. We were the same, but I thought I was right, and they were wrong, just like the residents of the west side of a mountain insisted that the mountain was East Mountain and those on the east side insisted it was West Mountain. After this realization, I was less critical of others. I came to realize that they are living in their own world, in the same way that I am living in mine. My attempts to spread the Buddha's teachings, rather than helping others, resulted in furthering my practice and enabling me to see my misperceptions about myself.

Since then, my attitude toward practice has changed significantly. Before, I used to read articles written by Buddhist scholars and taught Buddhist doctrine like a teacher instructing students. After my realization, I began to understand the true meaning behind the words in the sutras. Before, the content of the Diamond Sutra sounded hollow. I thought the text was too vague, "No existence, no non-existence, not this, not that..." Now I could understand the meaning of the text behind the words. It was like I could finally see the moon, not the finger pointing at the moon.

We all live inside our own misperceptions. I often say we need to be cautious of those who are regarded as good people. Why? Because those praised for being good stubbornly hold on to the thought that they are right. It's almost impossible to change their minds. On the other hand, those who are often subject to criticism are aware of their faults even though they may appear arrogant. Those who are often praised for being good believe they speak only the truth. Thus, they don't feel the need to reflect on themselves, and it's difficult for them to free themselves from any thoughts they are attached to. These are also the type of people who show blind faith in their religion. In Buddhism, being a good person is not praiseworthy. This doesn't mean you should be bad; it means a good person needs to be cautious because they can easily fall into ignorance. You need to become wise and come out of the well you've fallen into.

Awakening in Everyday Life

There is a story about the famous Jajang Yulsa.[*] Jajang Yulsa was one of the most eminent Buddhist monks during the Silla period. He prayed at Mt. Wutai, China, where he saw Manjushri, the bodhisattva of wisdom, in person. He received the precepts from Bodhisattva Manjushri, returned to Korea, and became the first patriarch of the Korean Vinaya School.[**]

---

[*]   Yulsa is a Korean title given to monks who specialize in the teaching of Buddhist precepts.

[**]   The Korean Vinaya School is a school of Buddhism that studies the rules of conduct for both monks and lay Buddhists.

When he met Manjushri at Mt. Wutai, he told Manjushri he hoped to see him again. Manjushri replied that he would see him on Mt. Taebaek after Jajang Yulsa returned to Silla. When Jajang Yulsa returned to Silla, he reorganized the Buddhist orders and became respected as a great teacher. In his later years, he resigned from leading the lineage and traveled with an attendant to Mt. Taebaek to see Manjushri one last time. He built a hut using vines on a slope of the mountain and devoutly prayed to see Bodhisattva Manjushri.

He began a one-hundred-day prayer. On the hundredth day, a man with long hair and wearing a monk's robe arrived at the temple. With an appearance that was neither monk nor layman and carrying a dead dog in a netted sack over his shoulder, he swaggered toward the place of prayer. It was taboo for any outsider to approach a sacred place of prayer, let alone someone carrying a dead dog. The attendant was horrified. Hoping to prevent bad luck, he immediately stood in front of the man to stop him and demanded he identify himself. The man pushed the attendant aside and shouted, "Is Jajang here? Is Jajang here?"

The attendant was flabbergasted. The man was being very rude, using Jajang Yulsa's first name when even the king treated him with respect. The attendant kept trying to push the man away.

"I have no business with you," the man told the attendant. "I am here to keep a promise I made. Get out of my way. Is Jajang here?" The man continued to shout the monk's name. The attendant finally calmed him down by assuring the man he would let him see the great master but just needed to ask him first. The attendant then went and told Jajang Yulsa about the man who had been shouting and making a commotion no matter how hard the attendant had tried to stop him. He told Jajang Yulsa that the man was insisting he was keeping a promise he'd made to the monk. After listening to the attendant, Jajang Yulsa said, "Maybe he's mad. Send him away."

Guess what the vagabond said when he heard this? "I will go away. I will go away. How could anyone who has the notion of self be able to see me?" He turned his netted sack upside down, whereupon the dead dog turned into a lion. The man mounted the lion, and they flew away to the east. When Jajang Yulsa heard this, he rushed out, running in the same direction the man had gone, calling out the name of Bodhisattva Manjushri, and passed away in the

When you are surrounded by the dark,
you must be able to discern
whether it is dark because there is no light
or because your eyes are closed.

process.

I'm not telling you this story to show how someone who had practiced as much as Jajang Yulsa failed to recognize Manjushri. I am telling you this story to explain that getting caught up in the notion of self is scary since even a great master like Jajang Yulsa wasn't able to recognize Manjushri because he was momentarily caught up in his thoughts.

Having the notion of self means getting caught up in one's thoughts. Where should you start to rid yourself of this notion? Begin with the idea that most of the thoughts you now have are subjective, so at the very least, you should not insist on them.

That should be the starting point. If you say you resolved not to get caught up in the notion of self, you will soon become caught up in the thought, "I'm not caught up in the notion of self," and this will create more problems. You need to accept that you're a being who can always get caught up in the notion of self, so just be aware of it and examine yourself instead of trying not to get caught up in that notion. Even if you can't free yourself from it, you should, at least, not insist on it. Then, even though your eyes are not open, you will no longer be yelling at someone to turn on the lights. When it's dark, you must be able to discern whether it's really dark, or your eyes are closed. If people say the lights are on, but it's still dark for you, you need to reflect on yourself and be aware that your eyes might be closed, instead of angrily demanding that someone turn on the lights. Only then can you open your eyes.

The same goes for the story of the wooden Buddha I mentioned earlier. We're always full of contradictions. But if we are aware of this, we can walk the path to awakening in our everyday lives without having to become a monk and renounce the world.

Hoejeong Sunim couldn't recognize Bodhisattva Avalokiteshvara even though he begged to see her. He said he'd do anything if the old man would just let him stay. But when the old man told him to marry his daughter, he refused, saying he couldn't break his vow of celibacy. Then, he was disappointed when he discovered that he couldn't consummate the marriage. His thoughts and actions were full of contradictions.

To see the embodiment of Avalokiteshvara isn't about meeting her in person. It's about realizing one's own contradictions in the process. Even though he failed to see

Avalokiteshvara, Hoejeong Sunim repented his ignorance and was able to return to his true nature. Therefore, the practice of self-reflection brings you a thousand times more blessings than saying a prayer asking for things you want.

You've Been Deceived
but You Don't Even Know It

A journalist asked Hoeam Sunim at Sundeoksa Temple, "Is there a paradise?" Hoeam Sunim smiled and answered, "The road outside the gate leads to Seoul."

In that very question, there is a hidden wish that the person wants to go to a good place after death. Hoeam Sunim's answer was that there was a road outside the gate that leads to Seoul. People might interpret his answer differently, but my interpretation is that he's saying there is no need to discuss whether there is a paradise or how we can get there. What we think, what we say, and what we do here and now, decide everything. There is no need to talk about Seoul, paradise, or elsewhere. In Seon Buddhism, this is often expressed by the saying, "Look under your feet."

There is a story related to this in *Samgukyusa*.* A king, along with noblemen and wealthy men, went to a memorial service held at a large temple. When the king was about to pass through the temple's "one-pillar gate," he noticed a monk in a threadbare robe standing at the entrance. Obviously, the monk was not allowed to enter because of his shabby attire. But the king ordered one of his attendants to let him in. After the service, the king told the monk, "You better not boast around that you went to a memorial service attended by the king." And the shabby-looking monk replied, "Your majesty, you better not brag that you went to a memorial service attended by the Buddha himself."

The surprised king watched as the monk flew away into the sky. He ordered his attendants to follow the monk. Since he was seen flying toward Mt. Namsan, they dismounted from their horses and started climbing the mountain. When they arrived where the monk had landed, they saw him place an alms bowl and a cane on top of a rock and then

---

* *Samgukyusa* is a book consisting of legends, folk tales, and historic accounts relating to the Three Kingdoms of Korea.

disappear. When they looked around, they found a small image of the Buddha engraved on a rock. The face of the image was identical to that of the monk they had just seen. The king, who sincerely repented, named the rock Seokgasa Temple. He also had a temple built where the alms bowl and cane had been left, and he named it Mubulsa Temple, which means "the place where the Buddha vanished." As this story reveals, you can't recognize the Buddha by his appearance.

Once upon a time, a hermit was invited to a feast. As many attendees were high-ranking officials and noblemen, the gatekeeper made judgments based on appearance and allowed entry only to those who were well dressed. Even though the hermit had been invited, the gatekeeper refused to let him in. After thinking about why this had happened, the hermit realized he was the only one who was shabbily dressed. He went home and changed into garments made of fine silk. When he returned, the gatekeeper greeted him politely and escorted him to a good seat.

The feast began, and all kinds of elegant food were served. When his glass was filled with wine for the toast, the hermit poured it on his clothes. He did the same with the food he'd been served. Needless to say, the other attendees were shocked by this behavior. They asked, "Why did you pour that wonderful wine on your good clothes? It was for you to drink, not to pour on your clothes." The hermit told them what had happened at the gate and then said, "I'm sitting here thanks to these clothes; therefore, it is not me but these clothes that should drink the wine and eat the food."

About ten years ago, I had a similar experience. A banquet hosted by the chairman of a large company was held at a luxury hotel in Seoul. I had been invited as one of the guests of honor. I was driven there by a member of the Jungto Society in her small car. Unfortunately, the concierge wouldn't let her car pull up at the hotel entrance, and I couldn't get out of the car.

It's not just about cars or clothes. Judging people based on external factors occurs quite frequently. Are the people in these stories the only ones who make such judgments? Every one of us judges others by their name, position, appearance, or career. That is how we are in our daily lives.

The following passage comes from the *Diamond Sutra*: "So, I say to you, this is how to contemplate our conditioned existence in this fleeting world:

Like a tiny drop of dew or
a bubble floating in a stream,
like a flash of lightning in a summer cloud,
or a flickering lamp, an illusion, a phantom, or a dream.
So is all conditioned existence to be seen."

All conditioned existence – that is, all forms, honor, and names – are like a dream, a phantom, a bubble floating in a stream, or a flickering lamp. They have no substance. They are like a tiny drop of dew or a flash of lightning. They are impermanent and quickly change. All conditioned existence needs to be viewed this way. We need to know that everything stays for a moment, and then disappears like a mirage because its nature is empty of self and is impermanent. If we understand this, we can live our lives without being fooled and believing otherwise. The problem is that this is almost impossible. Nevertheless, we need to stay aware so that we can recognize it immediately when we are being fooled. Then, we will be able to come to our senses.

PART 04

DEVELOP STRENGTH
THROUGH PRACTICE

Look inside yourself when you face a problem in life. Try looking at the problem from a new perspective rather than your habitual one. This will help you to live a life without being swayed no matter what happens. You may cry, but you won't be grief-stricken. You may laugh, but you won't be overly excited. You won't be shaken even though you become sick, grow old, or experience the death of a loved one. Only then can you say that you have attained peace and enlightenment.

You Don't Have to Believe It

I have a friend who lives in the United States. When I went to a U.S. city to give a Dharma talk, he called me. He said he had read about the event in the newspaper and wanted to see me. He showed up after the Dharma talk was over, when I was alone in the temple. I invited him to step inside, but he refused, saying that he couldn't enter a Buddhist temple because he was a Christian. So, we decided to go to his place. While we were casually chatting in his car on the way, he told me he was worried about something.

When I asked what was troubling him, he replied, "I'm an elder in my church, but I find myself unable to believe in God, no matter how many times I read the Bible. I have begun to envy those who believe in God after listening to a single sermon or reading the Bible just once. What should I do?"

"It is nothing to be concerned about."

"Do you have a solution for me?"

"Yes."

"What is it?"

"Just don't believe in God."

If you can't believe in God, you don't have to. There is absolutely no reason or need to believe in God. Similarly, in Seon Buddhism, practitioners make a fuss about not being able to practice a koan.* For all other people, whether you practice a koan or not is not a big deal. But for Seon practitioners, it's a huge problem. It's exactly the same as struggling to believe in God. They behave as if something horrific will occur if they can't practice a koan.

When we become caught up in our own thoughts, it's easy to think we are right and others are wrong or that my religion

---

* A koan is a story, dialogue, question, or statement which is used in Seon Buddhism to demonstrate the inadequacy of logical reasoning and to provoke enlightenment.

is right, and the religion of others is wrong. Similarly, we get caught up in the thought that our culture is superior to other cultures. If Buddhism did the same, there would be no need for Buddhism because it would be just one of many cultures, one of many thoughts, and one of many philosophies. There would be no need to practice Buddhism. Unfortunately, many Buddhists fail to follow the true teachings of the Buddha, so their minds are easily swayed, pursuing worldly power, profit, and fame.

There isn't much difference between a Christian who unsuccessfully tries to believe in God and a Seon practitioner who unsuccessfully tries to meditate on a koan. In the same way, a Buddhist who prays, "Dear Lord Buddha, please bless my family" is no different from a Christian who prays, "Dear God, please bless my family." The path to enlightenment lies in transcending concepts and looking at the realm of truth. Talking about practicing a koan is nothing more than knowledge-based imitation. If you truly believe in God, there is no way not to believe in Him, no matter how hard you try. If you are truly curious about something, you can't help but keep thinking about it, no matter how hard you try not to. That is what practicing a koan is. It's a koan when you can't stop thinking about it, whether you are awake or asleep, and whether you are sitting down or standing up.

Does a Dog Have Buddha-Nature?

A monk was sitting alone and meditating in the sun when he heard a rattling sound. Before starting his meditation, he had resolved to not move no matter what happened around him. However, he grew so curious about the rattling sound that he opened his eyes. He saw a dog chewing a fleshless bone, spitting it out, and then chewing on it again, repeating the same process over and over again. While observing this futile, repetitive action, he remembered a passage from a sutra: "All living beings have Buddha-nature."

This means that all living beings are Buddhas. If the dog was a Buddha, it was doing what a Buddha would do. As the monk watched the dog, its actions seemed like such a waste of time and effort. He couldn't believe it was something a Buddha would do. So, if it wasn't something a Buddha would do, the dog couldn't be a Buddha. And if the dog was not a Buddha, the sutra, which says that all living beings are Buddhas, would be wrong. Conversely, if the sutra were right, the dog's actions were what a Buddha would do. It seemed to him that a Buddha would never engage in such useless, repetitive action. Up to that moment, the monk had never doubted the phrase, "All living beings have Buddha-nature." So, he got up from his meditation pose and went to his teacher, and asked, "Teacher, does a dog have Buddha-nature?"

If the teacher had said yes, he would have accepted it, thinking a discriminatory thought had momentarily occurred in his head. But the monk was surprised by his teacher's answer. "You idiot, how can a dog have Buddha-nature?" These words left him dumbfounded. It was as if he'd been deprived of vision and hearing and was standing on the edge of a cliff. He was so stunned he didn't know whether the sun was up or down, whether he was eating or fasting, sleeping or awake, coming or going. "A dog doesn't have Buddha-nature? What does that mean?" he thought to himself. This is the moment the disciple began practicing a koan. Let's examine the situation more closely.

First, when the teacher said that a dog does not have Buddha-nature, the disciple would have wanted to refute the teacher's answer by citing the *Nirvana Sutra* that states all living beings have Buddha-nature. In other words, here, the disciple would be questioning the teacher's authority, which means he doesn't have trust in his teacher. In Seon Buddhism, the Dharma is transmitted between the teacher and the discipline, heart to heart, rather than through words. Without complete trust in the teacher, the disciple cannot attain enlightenment.

Second, let's say that the disciple holds an unwavering trust in the teacher. In this case, when the teacher told him that a dog doesn't have Buddha-nature, the disciple could assume that the words in the *Nirvana Sutra* must be wrong. Such distrust in the sutra means distrust in the Buddha's words. How can a practitioner attain enlightenment when he doesn't have faith in the Buddha's teachings?

The monk faced a dilemma. Believing the teacher's words that a dog has no Buddha-nature would mean distrusting the Buddha's teachings. On the other hand, believing the words of the sutra would mean distrusting his teacher. It was a problem whether he believed that a dog had Buddha-nature or whether he didn't, because either way, he wouldn't be able to attain enlightenment.

There is also a third way. When the teacher says that a dog doesn't have Buddha-nature while the *Nirvana Sutra* says it does, the monk may question, who is right? This is disbelieving both of them. So, the disciple neither trusts the teacher nor the Buddha's teachings. Most of us are at this level in our practice. We hear one thing here and another there, so we get confused and end up distrusting both. This is what we commonly do. Since we can't trust what someone says about the Dharma, we go ask someone else for clarification, which makes us confused and unable to believe what anyone says.

What Is This?

What happens if the disciple accepts both the words in the sutra and the teacher's answer?

The sutra says all living beings have Buddha-nature, but the teacher says that a dog doesn't. Belief doesn't cause confusion. When the teacher said that the dog doesn't have Buddha-nature, his answer wasn't about whether a dog does or doesn't have Buddha-nature. He answered that way to raise enough doubt in the disciple that the answer will make him seek the truth. "A dog doesn't have Buddha-nature? What does that mean? What does the teacher mean when he says a dog doesn't have Buddha nature?" The disciple can't figure out the answer to this question by studying the sutras. All the knowledge and information the disciple has held so far became useless due to his teacher's answer. That's why he felt as if he was deprived of vision and hearing. The statement, "A dog doesn't have Buddha-nature" would haunt the disciple no matter what he does, whether he was eating, going to the toilet, sitting or lying down. He searches for meaning beyond the existence or non-existence of Buddha-nature in a dog.

This is called truth-seeking. It's a new world where all traditional answers fail. Truth-seeking is similar to scientists researching a new principle. In science, this process is called research, while in Buddhism, it is called truth-seeking. In terms of travel, it's called exploration; it's exploring a new world. Since it's a new world that no one has ever been to and no one knows about, no one can say it's a certain way. You need to go there yourself to find out how it actually is. Just like an explorer in a new world or a researcher working on a new subject, a Seon practitioner needs to seek the truth by studying the meaning of "Mu" or "nothingness."

---

* Mu means "not" or "nothingness" and is an important concept in Seon Buddhism. It goes beyond "is" or "is not" to a place beyond all dualities, to being as it fundamentally is.

In truth-seeking, there is no other way other than experiencing it yourself. You can't understand it by asking questions and getting answers from others. There's no use asking people about the planet Venus when no one has ever been there. There's no use asking the question to others in the first place. It is meaningless to speculate about a place without traveling there yourself. This process can be compared to taking a step forward at the edge of a cliff. At the edge of the cliff, what is behind you is the world you know, and what is over the cliff is a new world no one has ever been to. You should just plunge into it.

Here is another analogy. How did Newton discover the law of universal gravitation? The story goes that one day he observed an apple falling to the ground and began investigating why apples always fell down. What would most people say if you asked them the same question? They'd say, "Gosh, where else would they fall? Upward? Sideways? What kind of question is that?"

Newton began to question what seemed so obvious to everyone else. He wondered why the apples fell down. Why don't they float up or travel sideways? Even when it's thrown sideways, an apple eventually falls down. When it's thrown straight up, the same thing happens – it comes back down. Newton thoroughly researched this phenomenon and discovered the principle of gravity: mass is subject to gravitational force. He also questioned whether there was a point of equilibrium between two objects where an object wouldn't fall. What would happen to an object so remote from earth it wasn't affected by the force of gravity? Through further research, Newton found that the earth moves around the sun and the moon moves around the earth. Like Newton, we need to ask important questions and investigate to find the answers ourselves.

The disciple needs to take such an approach to the teacher's answer that a dog doesn't have Buddha-nature. He needs to explore the meaning of "doesn't have" or "Mu" in depth, instead of simply accepting the answer. The process involves repeatedly experimenting, challenging, failing, and then challenging again. He has to keep trying. This is not about trying to believe in something he can't understand or struggling to meditate on a koan. He should raise a question so strong and profound that he can't set it aside, however much he tries. Then, "Mu" or "What is this?" becomes his koan.

In a nutshell, three things are critical for practicing Seon Buddhism. First, you need to have deep faith in the Buddha's teachings and the teacher's guidance. Second, you need to have a profound question or doubt. Third, you need to have a strong determination to find the answer. You have to be exasperated that you have yet to find the answer to the question. You may find yourself thinking, "How could I still not know the answer to this question? I'll get to the bottom of it, and nothing will stop me from finding the answer." This exasperation, which is different from being angry at someone, becomes a driving force in seeking the truth. Three things are essential to profoundly contemplate a koan: deep faith, profound doubt, and great determination.

A Question That Comes
Like a Bolt Out of the Blue

You brave rough roads and countless miles to reach a teacher. You open the door of the teacher's room, bow to him to ask a question, and the teacher roars, "What is this that came?"

For any other question you can find the answer in books or by asking others, but who can you ask when the question is "Who are you?" If you ask someone this question, he will probably think you're crazy. "Who am I?" What is this "I" that I constantly use to indicate myself? You need to seriously investigate what this "I" is.

To the question, "Who are you?" some people will answer, "Me? I am me. Who else would I be?" and the investigation ends right there. Other people might answer with the title of their occupation such as "I'm a monk," and if asked again, they would reply, "Who are you, then?" Rather than investigate who they themselves are, people become defensive or resistant to the question. They try to find fault with the question rather than trying to find out who they are.

In my experience, most people can't respond to this line of questioning more than three times. The dialog usually goes something like this: "Who are you?"

"I am Pomnyun."

"Is Pomnyun you or your name?"

"It's my name."

"I didn't ask you your name. Who are you?"

"Me? I'm a monk."

"Are all monks you?"

"No."

"Then, who are you?"

If I continue asking this question more than three times, they run out of answers. At that point, they begin to resist. They can't think of anything to say, so they start repeating, "I am me," or they fight back by asking me, "Who are YOU?" Everything they know becomes useless. They can't answer the question with what they know and are left with the realization that they have lived a hollow life, one that is out of touch with reality.

That's how most people are. However smart or arrogant people may act, if they lost their jobs, they would feel utterly lost. If those who have been leading a life of luxury suddenly lose all their wealth and go bankrupt, they would become completely dejected. If those who boast about being happy suddenly lost their spouse, parent, or child, they would be truly heartbroken. Some people may put on airs and boast about themselves, but if they were publicly disgraced or sent to jail after a journalist reveals their scandal, they would be totally dispirited. If those who talk confidently about their health are suddenly diagnosed with terminal cancer, they would be extremely distressed. The truth is that there is nothing people can confidently boast about.

Why are people like this? It's because they can't see the truth that lies behind this line of questioning, and they fail to go beyond three questions. They consider themselves to be someone they are not and consider something that is not theirs as theirs, so when what they thought were certainties disappear, their minds go blank. The things they considered

If the student believes his teacher
that a dog does not have the Buddha nature,
then he no longer believes in the Buddha.
If he believes the sutra
and thinks a dog has the Buddha nature,
then he no longer believes his teacher.

as part of themselves and commodities that were theirs are proven to be fake and imaginary. That's why we all need to deeply investigate our true nature.

But most of us are too lazy to do this. When I continue this line of questioning at the Awakening Retreat, the attendees usually can't come up with anything to say. Many people just keep repeating that they don't know. Those who definitely ask me back, "I am me. Who are you, then?" also keep repeating the same question. Quick-tempered people just get angry and say, "Why are you asking me that question? I didn't come here for this."

This question should strike you like lightning. It has to be a shock that makes you deaf and blind like a bolt of lightning, a shock that makes you focus only on this question. If you spend all your time waiting for the next meal or bedtime at the Awakening Retreat, you won't be able to realize anything. If all a monk does is wait for the end of the meditation when the striking of the bamboo stick signals the beginning of meditation, or if they think about the next meal after the bamboo stick signals the end of the meditation, they won't be able to attain any kind of awakening, no matter how many years they meditate.

A Taste of Enlightenment

When you light a match, you have to strike it hard to ignite it. Striking it gently won't be effective even if you do it 300 times. When you complain you can't start a fire even though you struck the match 300 times, someone will tell you to strike the match harder. When you do, the fire will start on your 301st attempt. Then, you may even instruct another person who has struck the match 10 times that they need to strike it at least 301 times to succeed. However, the number of times or even the hours spent aren't important. That's not how you are supposed to practice. You need to raise your own doubts. A monk can even practice a koan while watching a dog chewing a bone if he raises big doubts on whether dogs also have Buddha-nature.

Suppose you are so in love with your partner that you felt you couldn't live without them. However, if your partner has an affair, you'll no doubt become infuriated and scream, "How could you cheat on me? I'll kill you." If you can self-reflect at that moment, it could be an opportunity to practice a koan. You could investigate the matter by asking, "How did this happen?"

Obviously, there were many things you didn't know about your partner although you slept together in the same bed.

It's trite to judge your partner's actions based on whether they're right or wrong. If you start thinking, "What didn't I know about my partner?" the question becomes your research topic. You may raise questions like "What made my partner cheat on me? What is something my partner found lacking in me? Did my partner have an unfulfilled need?" If you are a practitioner, when something like this happens to you, a big question will take hold of your mind.

So, why don't you start studying your partner today? You could become a true expert on how a person's mind works and even be able to publish a book on it if you investigate deeply into your partner's mind. Someone who publishes a book by piecing together content from other people's work is not really an expert. Neither the author nor the reader would really understand the content of such a book. The same is true for Dharma talks. Some Dharma talks explain stories in the sutras using lots of commentaries, but it's hard to understand what they mean. They are not the living words of the Buddha. Therefore, such Dharma talks hardly move you or change your life. Some people show their devotion by reciting the *Diamond Sutra* seven times a day or chanting mantras 300 times a day, but they fail to change their lives in any way. Whether a Buddhist, Christian, atheist, chanter, or meditation practitioner, they are all the same in that they're likely to go crazy upon finding out their partner cheated on them. There is no difference.

"Mu" does not mean "non-existence" in the dualistic way of thinking about existence and non-existence. It's not a matter of choosing between existence and non-existence or discussing which is right between the two. It's a new realm beyond the dichotomy of existence and non-existence; it is the world of truth and the world of reality. It's called the true reality of all things. You have to see and experience it for yourself.

Until then, your life is a dream. Even though you say you know, you actually don't. While getting blown about in all directions like a fallen leaf on a windy day, you might end up abandoned and discarded in a gutter when the wind stops. You will likely live like this, not only in this life but also in many lives after this. Try deeply investigating "What is this?" just for a few days, and you will begin to know who you are.

Beyond This World

I was once invited to talk about Buddhism at a training program for the Christian clergy. They were respected clergymen who had started a movement to live like Jesus. They believed people's lives had become too estranged from the way Jesus lived his life and that people have forgotten the spirit of Christianity. I readily accepted the invitation. It was a wonderful opportunity as we were kindred spirits in search of the truth.

They had a special request for me: "Sunim, please don't just talk about Buddhism. Let us experience it. We are already very good at talking about things. Help us experience it physically rather than just talk to us about it."

This was not an easy thing to do, and I thought about it for several days. When they talked about experiencing Buddhism physically, I decided they meant they wanted to try doing Seon meditation, Vipassana meditation, or yoga practice. Are these things Buddhism? No, not really. But non-Buddhists often think they are. I felt that if I didn't include at least one of them in the program, they would say I had talked only about Buddhism instead of allowing them to experience it physically even if my words enabled them to experience something. I asked a professor, who was renowned as a top yoga practitioner, to help me. During the four-day training program, I was allotted six hours in total, two hours daily for three days. I divided the six hours equally with the yoga professor, so each of us had one hour per day to conduct our session. The clergymen told me they enjoyed the yoga class every morning even though they found it physically challenging.

When it came time for me to conduct my session, there were about 30 to 40 people sitting in a circle. The pastor sitting next to me was wearing a watch, so I started the session by asking him a question. "Reverend, what a nice watch! Whose watch is it?"

"It's mine."

"Is it really yours?"

"Yes, it is."

"Why is it yours?"

"Because I bought it with my money."

"You bought it with your money. But why is it yours?"

"Because I bought it with my money. Why do you keep asking me that?"

So, I asked him again, "Reverend, that watch. Who does it belong to?"

"Gosh. I told you it's mine. I'm a clergyman. Do you think I'd steal someone else's watch?"

"No. But why is it yours?"

"I already told you I bought it with my own money. I have its warranty certificate."

Once again, I asked him, "The watch you are wearing on your wrist, whose watch is it?"

"My goodness! I keep telling you it's mine. Why are you wasting the little time we have together by asking me such a meaningless question?"

"Why is it yours?"

"As I said, I paid for it with my own money. Do I need to show you where I bought it?"

"You bought it with money, but why is it yours?"

"It's mine because we live in a capitalistic society, and I bought it with my own money."

Pointing to a leather satchel, I asked the pastor sitting next to him, "Whose bag is that?"

"It's mine."

"Why is it yours?"

"My wife gave it to me as a gift when we got married."

"It was a present, but why is it yours?"

"Uh, it's mine because I got it as a present."

"Reverend."

"Yes?"

"Whose bag is it?"

"It's mine."

"Why is it yours?"

"I told you. I got it as a wedding gift."

"You got it as a present, but why is it yours?

"Because I received it as a present. Do you think it should be yours? Do you want it?"

"It's not a matter of whether or not I want it. I asked you

whose bag it is."

"Heavens! I'm telling you it's mine because it's mine. Why would I say it's mine if it isn't?"

The pastor sitting next to him was wearing a ring. So I asked him, "Reverend, whose ring is that?"

Everyone was dumbfounded. They whispered among themselves that I kept repeating the same question. They were thinking that I was wasting their precious time by asking the same question over and over again. Some of them left in the middle of the session. I just continued to ask questions about who the tie, suit, sock, etc. belonged to. They gave me all kinds of reasons why a particular item was theirs: they bought it, made it, found it, or someone gave it to them. In general, a person will ask a question once or twice and then stop. But as I kept asking the same question repeatedly, everybody was bored to death. When the time assigned to me was almost over and half the people had left, one of the clergymen suddenly exclaimed, "Hallelujah! God has blessed me!"

Everyone in the room stared at him. He exclaimed that he witnessed God's work through a Buddhist monk. He said, "Reverends, how can all these things be ours? They belong to God, the creator of all things."

All at once, the mood in the room turned solemn. When you think about it, he was correct. Christians preach that everything in this world, including every single strand of hair, is created by God. If that is true, how can there be anything that is mine or yours? Everything belongs to God. They had been preaching to their congregation that God created everything but then had stubbornly insisted that everything was theirs.

That's how contradictory we are. In theory, the clergymen believed that nothing was theirs; everything belongs to God. But when I asked them, the pastors kept insisting that those items belonged to them. When they answered me, they didn't have a single doubt that those items were theirs, but when they were preaching to their congregation, they didn't have a single doubt that everything was God's. How could they see God and hear His voice when they were so stubbornly insisting that those items belonged to them? Once they realized the inconsistency of their thoughts, the mood in the room totally changed. The clergymen realized they had been blind. They had insisted that the items were theirs with their eyes closed and had refused to see them even though I tried to show them the truth.

If I had wrapped up the session with this insight, my relationship with them would have remained good. They would have felt blessed, like seeing the sunlight breaking through the clouds and pigeons gracefully flying down from high up in the sky. But I continued to ask questions. "Whose is it?"

"It's God's."

"Why is it God's?"

"Because God created it."

"When you say God created it, you mean that God made it, right? If that's true, why don't cars belong to the workers who make them? Why is this God's just because He made it?"

"Those are two very different things. God created this world, so everything in it belongs to God."

"Why does it belong to God?"

"Because God created it."

"God made it, but why is it God's?"

People got stuck at that point. Even though they thought I was a strange monk, they tolerated me until they thought I was denying God altogether. From that moment on, they

A Taste of Enlightenment

stopped listening to me. Initially, they felt that they had been blessed to see the truth, but then I disturbed them with more questions.

The purpose of asking these questions wasn't to argue about whether something belonged to someone or not. This is as futile as arguing about the existence or non-existence of Buddha-nature. The actual purpose of my line of questioning was to help people experience a new realm beyond the world of "yours" and "mine." There is no evidence to prove that something actually belongs to someone, no matter how long we argue about it. They can only insist that the items belong to them because they made them or bought them.

Some resorted to defiantly redirecting the question back at me: "What about you? Whom does the watch you are wearing belong to?" In order to transcend the world of "yours" and "mine," we must examine this question deeply.

Talking about the codes of law and the basic principles in a capitalist society is useless. You have to step into a new world. At the edge of the cliff, you have to take a step forward. When you transcend concepts like "yours" and "mine," a bright new world of truth opens up. It's like opening the door of a dark room and stepping outside into the bright light. The realization, "Wow, that's how it is," is not the same as, "I see." It isn't about knowing something is mine, yours, or God's. The moment you realize, "That's how it is," all your afflictions disappear, and you feel peaceful. Everything becomes clear, like turning on the light in a dark room. You neither resist the question nor are you troubled by it. You can answer without hesitation even if you are questioned a hundred times without becoming bored by it. And you can finally see how stubborn people are and the way they close their eyes and scream about how dark the world is. You can't see these things until you are awakened.

Therefore, we need to break away from the world of illusion we're living in. At least once, we should experience removing the colored glasses that we didn't even know we were wearing all along. Otherwise, we'll never realize how lost we are in our dreams. We should at least know that it's a dream even if we continue dreaming. Likewise, when we watch a play, we should be aware that it's fiction even when we're moved to tears. We live our lives like drifting clouds, half asleep as if we are wandering in a dream. And this is why we make a fuss about trivial matters every day as if our lives depended on them.

Do You Know
That You Don't Know?

When we closely examine the things that seem clearly right or wrong, we find that they cannot be so strictly defined after all. Since the Five Precepts* are so clear, we think that we would immediately notice when we break one. However, in practice, it's not so simple. Let's say I drank a glass of soju.** Would this be breaking the precept of refraining from intoxicants? Yes, it would be. Why? Because I drank alcohol. But let's take a closer look. Let's say a glass of soju

---

* Five Precepts are the five basic rules of moral and ethical behavior for Buddhists.

** Soju is a Korean distilled liquor.

is 4 oz. If I drink just 2 oz., is it still considered breaking the precept? How about when I drink 0.4 oz. or 0.04 oz.? There's a popular health drink called Bacchus in Korea that contains 0.004 oz. of alcohol in each bottle. If I drank a bottle of Bacchus, would I be breaking the precept? If we analyzed everything this way, it would be hard for us to freely drink even a glass of water or juice.

On the other hand, what would happen if we said that it's okay to drink 0.4 oz. of alcohol? If that is allowed, what about 0.6 oz? Would that be okay? What about 0.8 oz or 1.2 oz? Then, soon it will become acceptable to drink a quart or even a gallon of alcohol.

This is not a simple question. In general, we say that, in order to abide by the precepts, no intoxicating beverage is allowed. However, there are people who have a very low tolerance for alcohol and become drunk on a bottle of a health drink, and there are others who are hardly affected after drinking a glass of beer. So, which group of people is the problem, the former or the latter? When you examine the issue in detail, things get even more complicated. Can we say that it's okay to drink as long as you don't become drunk? Then again, have you ever known anyone who admits to being drunk?

And how can you tell whether someone is drunk? Can you believe the words of someone who says they aren't drunk?

If you probe deeper, it becomes impossible to decide whether someone has or hasn't broken the precept based on whether or not they drank alcohol. This leads to a realm where we can't tell whether someone has actually broken the precept. In this realm, it doesn't make sense to say someone has broken it, but at the same time, it doesn't make sense to say someone hasn't. That's why we need to move to a world that transcends such judgments. From there, we need to return to the world where judgment is made on whether or not the precept was violated.

Let's take another example. A married woman spent a night with a man who wasn't her husband. Did she break the precept on abstaining from sexual misconduct? If we say that she did, what if she did nothing other than hug the man that night? What if she just held his hand? If we say those actions can be considered breaking the precept, then maybe being in the same room with a man who is not her husband could also be considered a violation of the precept. How about if they simply looked at each other? Did she break the precept or not? If we say she didn't break the precept, what if she touched him with her pinkie? Did she break the precept or not? What if she only touched his clothes with her hand? What if she just hugged him, and rubbed her cheeks against his? It's all the same. If we continue in this direction, we won't be able to draw a clear line between actions that violate the precepts and those that don't.

We can't decide this issue with the binary concept of "violation" or "non-violation" of the precepts. We have to proceed to the realm that transcends these ideas. Then we can come back and discuss whether or not a particular behavior constitutes a violation. In the same vein, we first have to move to the realm that transcends the concepts of "yours" and "mine" and then come back and discuss "yours" and "mine." Once we transcend the binary distinction, we can see that existence and non-existence are just words we use. Otherwise, it's all just a puppet show. We talk about things being yours and mine, or that someone broke or didn't break a precept, but we don't really know what we're talking about.

If you truly know that you don't know, you won't be able to say anything. If you really know that you actually don't know, you won't be able to say whether something is right or wrong. Your question will plague you like a fish bone stuck in your throat. You don't have the energy to trouble yourself with other people's business. In that state, you can only concentrate on the question, "What is this?" You can't help but focus on it, no matter what you're doing, whether it's sitting or standing, eating, or going to the restroom.

But how are most people practicing? You say you're meditating on a koan, but you keep forgetting about it while talking, sleeping, or walking. During koan meditation, you wait for the bamboo stick to strike, signaling the end of meditation. Or you doze off during the meditation, and you are busy going to the restroom, getting something to eat, or occupying yourself with other things. As a result, no matter how long you meditate on a koan, you fail to solve it. How nice it would be if something became yours simply because you insist that it is. However, in reality, that's not possible.

Let's say you were in a traffic accident, and you're about to die. At that moment the clasp of the watch you so stubbornly insisted was yours breaks, and the watch falls to the ground. At that moment, whose watch is it? Is it still yours after you die? We live under such misconceptions. We can only wake up from a dream when we become aware that we are dreaming. Even if we can't wake up, we won't be fooled as long as we know it's a dream.

Therefore, we should seriously investigate the truth rather than live groundlessly. When you see a phenomenon, you have to make an effort to find its essence. However, we humans are lazy. Lazy thinking is a force of habit. When we live according to our habits, every day is the same.

If we don't know something, we need to study and learn about it. If we don't know the answer when someone asks us a question, we will only find out when we ask someone else or search for the answer on our own. In this sense, not knowing isn't a bad thing. It's actually a good thing because then we can learn something new. If we keep trying, even when all the things we know are proven useless, we will realize something new. We will get to know a whole new world. Instead of lamenting about our fate and our suffering, we should face life head-on.

I once advised someone to attend the Awakening Retreat, and that person said, "Sunim, one of my friends attended it but they haven't changed in any way." Well, how much can a person change after a few days of reflection? But actually, that's not necessarily the case. Even though your friend may act the same, their world may have changed. Even though your friend may suffer and get confused just like any other person, their world has changed. No one can judge another person's life. When you taste such a world even once, you can expand on it. If you haven't experienced it yet, you need to. Those who haven't experienced it have no clue that such a world exists. Even those who have experienced a taste of it can only maintain it for a little while. Then, they become lost again, and the world of truth feels like a dream. It's like waking up momentarily and then falling back to sleep again. Your dream becomes reality, and the awakening you experienced a short time ago becomes the dream. You are lost again, remembering how nice that dream was.

You need to practice more earnestly. Your life itself is a koan. You have to closely examine the things you face in life. Do not let habits determine how you react to them. Study them with fresh eyes. That's when you'll be able to live a life that is not shaken, no matter what happens. You won't be grief-stricken even though you cry. You won't be euphoric even though you laugh. You won't be shaken even though you become sick, grow old, or lose a loved one. Only then can you say you've attained peace and enlightenment.

PART 05

PRACTICE IN YOUR DAILY LIFE

If you fall into the water, instead of flailing helplessly and screaming for help, search for a pearl. If you're married, have a child, go bankrupt, have cancer, or grow old, instead of suffering, look for opportunities to be awakened. There are things you can realize only when you are old, sick, divorced, or have been betrayed. Wonhyo Daesa attained enlightenment when he vomited the water he drank from a skull. Awakening is not far away. Awakening is wherever your mind arises. You can attain nirvana in a single moment, or you can wander around in the six realms of existence life after life.

Realizing That Dirtiness and
Cleanliness Are Not Two Different Things

Wonhyo Daesa* came from a noble family of the Silla Kingdom. The highest class in Silla were the royals, followed by the nobility, called Yukdupum,** the commoners, and finally the lower class. People of the low class resided in specific slum areas called So and Bugok. The crown and most of the kingdom's vital positions were held by members of the royal family. The nobility was forbidden to hold positions above a certain level. The great leaders and philosophers of

---

* Wonhyo Daesa was an honorary Korean term used for renowned Korean monks.

** Yukdupum are descendants of the chiefs of the six tribes.

any society often come from the second highest class, since the highest class has a vested interest in maintaining the status quo, and doesn't see the existing social contradictions. On the other hand, lower-class people can't afford to search for the truth, as they are too busy trying to make ends meet. They either obey or resist societal norms, but they don't have the power or time to create a new order.

Maybe because Wonhyo Daesa was a member of the nobility and not the royal family, he was able to develop eyes that could discern the existing social contradictions. He came from a wealthy family, but, after his parents died when he was a young boy, he was raised by his grandparents. Like most noblemen of the time, during their teens, he became a Hwarang,* a member of an elite group of young males in Silla. As he was smart, good-looking, and a nobleman, he was on a fast track to the top.

At that time, Silla was continuously at war with its neighboring kingdoms: Goguryeo and Baekje. Wonhyo Daesa, along with other young Silla Hwarangs, willingly participated in the wars, fighting against Silla's enemies.

---

* Hwarang, also known as Hwarang Corps, and Flowering Knights, were an elite warrior group of male youth in Silla.

Wonhyo Daesa's fame increased as he continuously won battle after battle. Then, his best friend was killed in a battle, and he was grief-stricken. Standing at his friend's grave, he swore to avenge his friend's death no matter what.

The minute he vowed revenge, a memory flashed through his mind of how he had jumped with joy while grasping the head of an enemy commander. Then, he thought about how his enemies must be cheering their victory while he was vowing to avenge the death of his best friend. And conversely, his enemies must have mourned the death of their comrades, vowing to avenge them while he had been celebrating his victory over them. That's when it became clear to him: there can only be winners because there are losers. All at once, Wonhyo Daesa experienced a profound realization. He realized how meaningless and how futile winning or losing was. So, he left the military and became a Buddhist monk. He shaved his head, transformed his house into a temple, and concentrated on practicing the Buddha's teachings.

This was Wonhyo Daesa's first awakening. Up until that point, he saw only from his own perspective, but now, for the first time, he began to see from other people's perspectives. It's like a Korean being able to understand the perspective of a Japanese, a South Korean being able to see the perspective of a North Korean, the husband being able to understand the perspective of his wife, or an employer being able to understand the perspective of the employees.

How did he attain his first awakening? It happened the instant he understood the other person's position rather than just his own. At that moment, he realized that arguing about you or me, winning or losing, or being right or wrong was an exercise in futility.

However, we still live our lives thinking only about ourselves. The wife, the husband, parents, children, employers, and employees, all only see from their own perspectives. It's the same with nations: South Korea, North Korea, and Japan only see things from their respective positions. This is the notion of self. As long as we remain imprisoned inside our own perspectives, we can't see the truth. We can't see the different sides of the same situation.

But Wonhyo Daesa awakened to reality, the truth of things, when he saw the other person's position as well as his own. When he became enlightened, he realized that the notion of self was utterly futile. The notion of being right or wrong and winning or losing was like a midsummer night's dream. You can realize the dream is meaningless only after you awaken from it. Before you wake up, you don't realize how futile everything is. After Wonhyo Daesa clearly understood that all the fixed notions in life were meaningless and that life was like a dream, he no longer felt the need to remain in the secular world. Those who become monks without such an awakening continue the futile argument of things being right and wrong. However, Wonhyo Daesa realized on his own that the riches and honors of the secular world were ephemeral and fleeting. There is a big difference between practicing after attaining enlightenment on their own like Wonhyo Daesa and practicing half-heartedly while remaining attached to the secular world.

Wonhyo Daesa practiced diligently after he became a monk. When he studied the Buddhist sutras extensively, he saw for himself that the Buddha had already attained enlightenment and realized the truth of all things 2,000 years earlier. He wondered why he hadn't known about this wonderful Dharma and had rummaged through the trash when a sumptuous meal had been laid out for him all along. Once he had a taste of the Dharma, he lost his appetite for everything else, so he practiced tirelessly, reading all the sutras and commentaries that were available in the country. However, at the time only a fraction of Buddhist sutras was available in Silla. Not all Buddhist sutras in India had been translated into Chinese, and only a few of those had been brought into Silla. There were many more translated sutras available in China, which was under the rule of the Tang dynasty.* So, as a seeker of truth, it was only natural for him to travel to China.

It was difficult for the people in Silla to go to Tang at the time, mainly due to the conflicts among the three Korean kingdoms: Silla, Goguryeo, and Baekje. The overland route was blocked by Goguryeo while the marine route was blocked by Baekje. Unless the Silla government arranged a ship to Tang for official purposes, it was very difficult for people to travel there by sea. At great risk to their lives, Wonhyo Daesa and Uisang Daesa, his fellow practitioner, made plans to go to Tang via Goguryeo to study the Dharma. Unfortunately, they were captured by Gogureyeo border guards while crossing the border. As Goguryeo and Silla were at war, they were mistaken for spies disguised as

---

* The Tang Dynasty was an imperial dynasty of China that ruled from 618 to 907 AD.

monks, not such a farfetched assumption. This left the two monks facing the possibility of execution.

When a higher-ranking guard, who might have been a Buddhist, investigated the monks, he was unable to find any evidence that they were spies. But the guard's rank did not give him the authority to release them, so one night he left their prison door open, so they could escape. He handled it this way in the hope that he wouldn't be held accountable for their escape. As a result, the two monks returned to Silla safely.

As his attempt to reach Tang had almost killed him, Wonhyo Daesa could have chosen to give up, but his passion for the Dharma was too strong. He decided to try again, this time using the marine route. This was the route that Silla had used to request help from the Tang Dynasty when Baekje and Goguryeo had invaded Silla in the past. This was the reason that Wonhyo Daesa decided to travel to Tang by sea. For several days, he wandered the docks, searching for a ship setting sail to Tang. One day, without warning, a storm broke. Quickly he was drenched by the downpour. Searching for shelter nearby, he discovered an opening to a cave.

Inside, the cave was pitch black; he couldn't see a thing. When he grew thirsty, he had to grope around until he felt a gourd-like object near him on the floor, which he used to collect rainwater. The water he drank tasted sweet and quickly quenched his thirst. Then, he grew drowsy and fell sound asleep. The next morning, however, he awoke to discover that the gourd he'd drunk from the night before wasn't a gourd at all but a skull. The moment he recognized his drinking vessel for what it actually was, he became nauseous and vomited. It was at that moment he attained enlightenment.

Wonhyo Daesa thought to himself, "The night before the water had tasted sweet, so why was it disgusting this morning? Was it a different vessel? No. It was the same one I had drunk from. Was the water different? No. The water was the same. Both the vessel and the water were the same, so why did the water that tasted so sweet the night before make me nauseous this morning? It was because I believed the water from the night before was clean, and, today, I believed it was dirty. However, the water and the vessel are the same." So, he realized that the perception of dirtiness and cleanliness arose from within him. Dirtiness and cleanliness did not exist in the vessel or water; they existed in his mind. "All phenomena arise and disappear depending on the mind." This realization made him so happy, that he danced for joy.

There are different versions of the story of Wonhyo Daesa's enlightenment. According to another version, he took shelter in a cave where he slept well, but in the morning discovered he wasn't in a cave but in a tomb. That realization kept him from sleeping the following night because every time he closed his eyes, ghosts appeared in his dreams. At that moment, he realized that before he knew it was a tomb he had slept soundly, but after his discovery, he became uneasy. The thought of sleeping in a tomb raised a number of disturbing emotions in his mind. The place was the same, but he'd slept soundly yesterday. Today, though, he felt agitated and was unable to sleep, so he realized that the concept of holiness and unholiness all existed in his mind.

Whichever version is true, the main point remains the same:

When one thought arises,
all phenomena arise.

When one thought disappears,

all phenomena disappear.

The three realms of existence* are all in the mind,

and all phenomena are the result of perception.

There is no Dharma outside of the mind.

Where else would you seek it?

The Dharma was not in China, India, or the sutras. It's in the mind, and there's no need to search for it anywhere else. Deciding there was no need to go to China after this realization, Wonhyo Daesa returned to Seorabeol, the capital of Silla. However, his friend, Uisang Daesa, traveled to China where he studied under Zhiyan, the second patriarch of the Huayan School of Chinese Buddhism. He came back to Silla and became the first patriarch of the Hwaeom School of Korean Buddhism. In today's terms, Uisang Daesa was an internationally educated monk, whereas Wonhyo Daesa was a domestically educated monk.

From that point on, Wonhyo Daesa read all types of sutras. There was nothing he could not understand, because all the

---

* the world of desire, the world of form, and the world of formlessness

teachings in the Mahayana sutras point to the idea found in the *Heart Sutra*: "Form is emptiness, and emptiness is form."

In other words, all phenomena are empty, meaning that everything exists in the mind, and the mind has no substance. After he attained enlightenment, Wonhyo Daesa wrote many commentaries on the sutras and Buddhist doctrines, which were profound but easy to understand at the same time. Everyone who read them was greatly impressed. Dharma talks on the same sutra can be easy or difficult to understand, depending on the person giving the talk. Some people simply interpret the words of the sutra, while others explain what those words mean with various examples from everyday life, making them easier to understand.

Turning Away from Sentient Beings

Owing to his abundant knowledge and wisdom, Wonhyo Daesa very quickly became famous. He was revered as one of the greatest scholars in Silla and, later, was favored by Queen Seondeok (Reign: 632-647), and became the abbot of Bunhwangsa Temple.

One day, while he was returning to the temple, he encountered Daean Daesa, a traveling monk who wasn't as well-known as Wonhyo Daesa, and whose origins were unclear. The traveling monk was called Daean Daesa because Daean is what he would shout on his alms round. The word "Dae" means big or great and the word "An" means peace, so what he was shouting was, "Everyone be at great peace."

After Jajang Yulsa became patriarch of the Buddhist lineage in Silla, a system of precepts was established, so rules of conduct, as well as an organizational system for Buddhist monks were firmly established. At the time, most of the monks came from the royal family. As the court protected and supported Buddhism, the religion quickly spread and gained power. Many monks traveled to China to study Buddhism, and when they came back, they exerted significant influence on society.

While Buddhism spread rapidly, it also started colluding with political powers. In criticism of such corruption, a Buddhist grassroots movement began to emerge. The monks leading this movement were from the lower classes, so they were barred from rising to high ranks since the class system at that time was extremely rigid. While the Buddha had totally abolished the class system in the Sangha, Silla had failed to do the same. As a result, many great monks from the lower classes were not given due recognition in society. There are many stories of such monks in *Samgukyusa*.*

---

* *Samgukyusa* is a collection of legends, folktales, and historical accounts relating to Korea's Three Kingdoms.

Daean Daesa lived in seclusion and did not belong to mainstream Buddhism. Despite his accomplishments, he was not honored as an eminent monk within Buddhist circles, but Wonhyo Daesa respected him. One day, they ran into each other on the street, one a young high-ranking monk recognized by the king and his court, the other an elderly highly accomplished monk unrecognized by the world. Daean Daesa praised the much younger monk for his wonderful books filled with wisdom. When Daean Daesa wanted to talk further, Wonhyo Daesa accepted his invitation. He followed Daean Daesa as he crossed the Bukcheon stream behind Bunhwangsa Temple and entered a slum inhabited by people from the lower class. As it was the custom for noblemen to avoid such places, Wonhyo Daesa was uneasy. He'd never been to such a place before.

Daean Daesa led him to a tavern where he casually told the barman that he'd brought an important guest and that the barman should bring them drinks and food. Wonhyo Daesa was a well-known Buddhist monk. How could he sit in such an unholy place while so many people were watching him? He decided that this was not an appropriate place for him. He stood up and quickly left the tavern. As he left,

Daean Daesa asked him where he was going. When he kept walking without responding, Daean Daesa shouted, "Where are you going when the sentient being* who needs to be liberated is here?"

Daean Daesa's words shocked Wonhyo Daesa to his core. Mahayana Buddhism was all about liberating sentient beings. Its main philosophy was that there was no difference between dirtiness and cleanliness. In other words, it's the philosophy of emptiness. However, disconcerting thoughts rose within him, such as "This village is inhabited by the lower class. This is a tavern. This is an unholy place. This is a place I shouldn't be in." Thoughts like "This person is from the lower class" or "This is a dirty place" go against the Buddha's teachings. He was intimately familiar with all the Buddhist sutras, but when he was faced with these particular external circumstances, his mind had not functioned the way he wanted it to. He was totally shocked by his own behavior. He knew that everything was empty, yet he still differentiated between right and wrong, clean and dirty. He'd turned away from the sentient beings in front of him

---

* Sentient beings are those with consciousness and, therefore, capable of experiencing suffering.

because he'd judged them as dirty. How could he ever liberate sentient beings while he thought that way?

Shocked by Daean Daesa's words, he reflected on his thoughts and behavior and realized how pathetic they were. He wondered how he could claim he was a practitioner when he'd acted that way. So, he abandoned his position as the abbot of Bunhwangsa Temple and disappeared. He decided to practice the bodhisattva's way of life rather than simply possess knowledge of it. He disguised himself and became a menial worker for a large temple with hundreds of monks.

At that time, manual laborers at big temples belonged to the lower class. While the Buddha had abandoned class and gender-based discrimination, most monks in Silla came from noble families and had never worked a day in their lives. All physical work was performed by slaves or people from the lower class. While the temples were supposed to be above secular ways, the only reason the monks could practice in such comfort was because members of the lower class performed all the necessary physical labor. In addition to giving land to temples with prominent monks, the state also gifted them with slaves, and the temples relied on the wealth accrued from their labor. In other words, even the most eminent monks couldn't avoid the fundamental social order of a feudal society.

Just like the society of Silla was bound by the limits of feudal society, present-day Buddhism in Korea is bound by the limits of capitalism. Paid workers are necessary to maintain a temple. We might find nothing wrong with this, but future generations may judge that present-day Korean Buddhism operated within the capitalist system. This is the same way we believe that Buddhism in the Silla and Goryeo periods was bound to the class system of a feudal society.

Wonhyo Daesa voluntarily became one of the menial workers who served the monks. There was a social hierarchy even among the menial workers, and the senior workers abused Wonhyo Daesa. But since he'd become a menial worker to lead a bodhisattva's way of life, he endured the physical and verbal abuse of the senior workers and concentrated on his practice.

Who Are the Sentient Beings?

Wonhyo Daesa practiced the bodhisattva way of life: sweeping the yard, splitting firewood, heating rooms, cooking food, and working in the fields.

Then one day he overheard the monks in the most advanced level of study discussing *The Awakening of Faith in the Mahayana*, which is thought to be the most difficult of all the sutras. The monks were fiercely debating among themselves when Wonhyo Daesa, who was cleaning the wood floor, overheard the conversation. He realized that their interpretation of the sutra was totally wrong. Without thinking, he interrupted them, saying that it meant something else. The monks became irate that a servant, whose only purpose was to perform manual labor, had dared to interrupt their debate. Wonhyo Daesa, who immediately realized his mistake, saw how angry the monks were becoming. Quickly, he begged for their forgiveness.

The monks went to their teacher, explaining that they didn't understand what the sutra meant, and they begged him to explain it. The teacher, in turn, gave them the *Treatise on The Awakening of Faith in the Mahayana*, which had been written by Wonhyo Daesa. The monks read the book and were able to understand the difficult sutra easily and clearly. Then, it occurred to them that the explanation in the book was identical to the one the servant had given them earlier. They grew suspicious, and looking back, it struck them that there was something peculiar about the servant. They were aware that Wonhyo Daesa had recently disappeared, so they wondered if the servant was Wonhyo Daesa. They decided to look into it the following day.

In the meantime, at the temple, there was a monk who was a hunchback. He didn't take his meals with the other monks, but instead came to the kitchen to ask for food after mealtime was over. Even the servants thought he was annoying and looked down on him. But Wonhyo Daesa was compassionate toward the monk. He took good care of him even though others were mean to him. Wonhyo Daesa put food aside for him, gave him the crispy rice crust when he asked for it, and generally watched out for him. Since this monk always carried a jingling bell with him, he was called Bangwool Sunim.

That night, suspecting he'd given his identity away, Wonhyo Daesa tried to sneak out of the temple while everyone else was asleep. As he was leaving, Bangwool Sunim, who lived in the quarters next to the gate, opened the door of his room and said, "Goodbye, Wonhyo." At that moment, Wonhyo Daesa had a profound awakening.

Wonhyo Daesa had not recognized Bangwool Sunim, but Bangwool Sunim had recognized him. This was the same way that the monks in the lecture hall had not recognized Wonhyo Daesa, but he had recognized all of them. Bangwool Sunim had been watching Wonhyo Daesa's every move since he'd arrived at the temple with the intention of practicing the bodhisattva's way of life while keeping his identity hidden.

Bangwool means a jingling bell in Korean.

What do you think Wonhyo Daesa's sudden insight was? It was the realization that he had misunderstood Daean Daesa's advice all along. Daean Daesa had asked him, "Where are you going when the sentient being who needs to be liberated is here?" Wonhyo Daesa had thought that Daean was saying, "You say that cleanliness and dirtiness are not two different things and that you want to liberate all sentient beings, but you seem to consider the lower class people at the slum dirty, and you disregard them. What do you mean you want to liberate sentient beings?" However, Wonhyo Daesa finally realized that he had been mistakenly looking for sentient beings outside his own mind. What Daean Daesa had actually meant was that Wonhyo Daesa's mind, the one that had made the judgment, "This is a slum. This is a tavern. I shouldn't be in such an unholy place," was the mind of a sentient being. Daean Daesa meant that Wonhyo Daesa should examine his own mind.

Until then, Wonhyo Daesa thought of Bangwool Sunim as a pitiful sentient being, so he cared for him and treated him with compassion. However, Bangwool Sunim was not a pitiful sentient being. Just like he'd pitied someone who doesn't need pity, Wonhyo Daesa had been trying to liberate sentient beings who were not actually sentient beings because he mistakenly thought they were. Wonhyo Daesa finally attained enlightenment.

A Life Not Obstructed by Anything

Wonhyo Daesa attained total freedom. He returned to So and Bugok, the slum where the lower classes resided. But this time, he wasn't going there to liberate them. The truth is that there is no sentient being to liberate. The mind that judges something as right or wrong and clean or dirty is that of a sentient being, and the moment you possess such a mind, you become a sentient being. The people living in those places were already Buddhas; he did not go there to liberate them but to learn from them. With a humble heart, he went there to learn. When he'd gone to the temple to work as a menial worker, he thought, "I have a responsibility to save sentient beings, but I've been avoiding it because I feel uneasy being among them. But I will get up the courage to go to them." Now, he realized that there were no sentient beings he needed to liberate. With this realization, he went to the slum without any qualms. He went there to become friends with them, spend time with them, and learn from them.

But there was one problem. The people living in the village viewed him only as the great Wonhyo Daesa. They looked up to him. Before, he couldn't become friends with them because he looked down on them. Now, he couldn't be their equal because they put him on a pedestal. Before, he had been the problem, but were the villagers now the problem? It's easy to conclude that way, but it would go against the truth that all phenomena arise in the mind.

How could he solve this conundrum? Before, he had to change his views, but this time, he needed to alter people's perceptions of him. Wonhyo Daesa, who had truly become free, immediately grasped the heart of the problem. He needed to get rid of the delusion of "Wonhyo Daesa, the celebrated monk" because he was the one who had created this illusion.

That's when Wonhyo Daesa intentionally created a scandal

A Taste of Enlightenment

with Princess Yoseok.* What do you think happened after Wonhyo Daesa got intoxicated and fooled around with the princess and got her pregnant? People who had respected Wonhyo Daesa and held him in esteem changed their opinion quickly and viewed him as a scoundrel. In addition, Wonhyo Daesa began calling himself Soseong Geosa, which means "humble layman." He no longer claimed he was a monk after his son, Seolchong, was born. However, we continue to call him Wonhyo Daesa to this day.

Because Wonhyo Daesa abandoned his social status as a respected monk and was publicly denounced, he became an object of pity. Even the lower-class people started to feel sorry for him. So, they gladly took care of him and hung around with him. He was finally able to become friends with them as an equal. He sang and danced with them, beating a gourd just as they did instead of reciting sutras and beating a moktak like a respectable monk.

Wonhyo Daesa began to beat the gourd when he saw people staying wide awake and enjoying themselves as a clown performed, whereas many people dozed off when he

---

* Princess Yoseok was the daughter of King Muyeol of Silla, who had a son named Seolchong with a prominent Buddhist monk, Wonhyo Daesa.

gave Dharma talks. Accordingly, he started giving Dharma talks in the fashion of a clown. He composed a song about the Buddha's teachings while beating a gourd. In today's world, this would be the equivalent of singing a pop song while dancing. The song was called *A Song of No Obstruction* and the dance *A Dance of No Obstruction*. He spread the Buddha's teachings to the lower-class people by entertaining them with this song and dance.

At the time, Buddhism was the religion of royalty, and the nobility and had little to do with the common people. But Wonhyo Daesa spread Buddhism among the common people in a way they could easily understand. Thanks to Wonhyo Daesa, most of the common people, who were illiterate, were able to learn the Buddha's teachings just by chanting "Namo Amitabha," a homage to Amitabha Buddha, or "Namo Avalokiteshvara," a homage to Bodhisattva Avalokiteshvara.

Wonhyo Daesa no longer belonged to any class. He no longer had any character, role, or position to indicate that he was Wonhyo Daesa. When a monk cleans a Dharma Hall, we say that the monk is cleaning. But that isn't accurate. He becomes a cleaner when he cleans. He becomes a farmer when he farms. When a monk sells things, he is a merchant rather than a monk. This is the same as "Do not get attached even to pure self-nature. Manifest according to causes and conditions," which is written in *The Song of Dharma Nature*, an abstract of the *Flower Ornament Sutra* by Uisang Daesa. Just as water changes its shape according to its container, we shouldn't attach ourselves even to pure self-nature but simply manifest according to causes and conditions. Wonhyo Daesa filled all kinds of roles according to the causes and conditions because he did not insist on any fixed identity. This is called "ceaseless manifestations." There are many temples and caves in Korea that are said to have been built by Wonhyo Daesa, and there are many places where he practiced. Just as there was nothing that could be called Wonhyo Daesa, there was nothing that couldn't be called Wonhyo Daesa either. He was everywhere but was nowhere.

There is an anecdote about Wonhyo Daesa's actions based on the idea of no obstruction. When the mother of a friend, a snake catcher, passed away, this friend asked Wonhyo Daesa to assist him with her funeral. As the snake catcher belonged to the lower class, his mother's body was wrapped in a straw mat instead of being placed in a casket. He and

Wonhyo Daesa carried her to a grave site, dug a hole, and buried her. Then, the snake catcher asked, "Since you used to be a monk, could you chant a Buddhist prayer for my mother?" Wonhyo Daesa chanted a short Buddhist prayer: "Never be born; dying causes suffering. Do not die; being born causes suffering." He was chanting about liberation from reincarnation, which is nirvana. In the middle of his chanting, his friend interrupted, "That's too long. Say it in one word." So, Wonhyo Daesa replied, "Saeng-sa-go," which means "Living and dying are suffering." This satisfied his friend who said, "Now, you're doing it right." This is one example that shows Wonhyo Daesa's unhindered life.

Awakening Can Happen
the Moment the Mind Arises

Through Wonhyo Daesa's life, we can see the stages of enlightenment. In the *Flower Ornament Sutra*, the life of a layman who only pursues wealth and honor is called the realm of phenomena. This is the mundane world, the world where phenomena are considered real even though they are as ephemeral as bubbles. Behind this realm's manifested forms lies the world of essence, referred to as the realm of principle.

Wonhyo Daesa grasped the essence of beings the moment he began looking at others instead of only at himself. At first, he lived in the realm of phenomena. Then he moved on to the realm of principle, in other words, to the realm of truth. Fascinated by the world of truth, he studied it even at the risk of his own life. When he drank water from the skull in the tomb, he realized that phenomena and principles were not separate elements. He also realized that dirtiness and cleanliness were not separate concepts. This is called the realm of the non-interference between principle and phenomena. But soon, he transcended its boundary again, to the realm of mutual non-interference among phenomena.

There are four stages of enlightenment or four worlds. The first is the world of beings who are influenced by the dirtiness around them. Those belonging to this world become lazy when they are in the company of people who are lazy; they learn to curse when they're hanging out with those who curse; they steal when they are with people who steal; and they fight when they are among those who fight.

Existence within the second world is similar to the concept of not hanging around with the wrong crowd. This is the stage where you leave the impure world so that you don't get dirty. You enclose yourself within high walls and only stay in the pure world.

The third world is where one doesn't get dirty even when

surrounded by filth. This is the world of a lotus flower that blooms in the mud, but doesn't become soiled. Those belonging to this world do not smoke even in the company of smokers, don't drink alcohol even when they are with people who do, don't lie even when they're in the company of people who lie, and are not lazy when they're with people who are lazy. In other words, they're not influenced by their surroundings.

The fourth world is where one becomes a rag that wipes away the dirt. Those in this world don't care about getting dirty because that's how others get clean. They become the mud that makes the lotus flowers bloom. They hang out with thieves and liars, even stealing and lying with them, but those thieves and liars soon find themselves no longer wanting to steal or lie. For example, when a band of thieves abducted Wonhyo Daesa, after some time, they all ended up renouncing the world and became monks. This is the realm of mutual non-interference among phenomena.

Let me give you another analogy. The realm of phenomena is the world where people scream for help when the boat they took out to the ocean for a fun trip capsizes due to a storm. They intended to have fun but ended up struggling for their lives. These are sentient beings. They cry for help. Sometimes they may complain that they are miserable due to their spouses even though they got married to be happy, that they are unhappy because of their children despite the fact that they had children to be happy, and they are desperate because of their business which has gone bankrupt although they started it to make money and be happy.

The second world is where people build a strong seawall and only stay within the enclosed area, lest their boat gets capsized when they're out at sea. If you don't get married, don't have a child, or don't start a business, you will not suffer because of them. This is the world of principle. If you view it from a broader perspective, those floundering in the sea are caught between the waves, and those staying in the boat are locked inside the walls they built.

The third world is where they build a ship so formidable that they can safely sail the sea regardless of the weather. The ship won't be wrecked no matter how severe the storm, enabling them to freely enjoy their journey. This is the world of the bodhisattva, the realm of non-interference between phenomena and principle.

What do you think is the common factor among these

three worlds? It's the aim of not falling into the water. The first world is the worst since they have already fallen into the ocean. As for the second, they never even venture into the sea for fear they might fall into the water. In the third world, they build ships large enough to keep them safe. The large ship is a metaphor for the great aspiration that allows people to move about freely in the storm. However, in that case, you only have the freedom to avoid falling into the water; you don't have the freedom to fall into the water. So, either you don't go out to sea, or you need a large ship.

People belonging to the fourth world harvest pearls when they fall into the water. In this realm, there is no desire to avoid falling into the water. Whether they are on a large or small boat, the inhabitants of this world enjoy the sea. If they fall into the water, they harvest pearls. We don't say that a diver plunging into the water to harvest clams is falling into the water. However, in truth, that's exactly what they do. But once there, they don't struggle. This is the realm of non-interference among phenomena, the world where one enjoys unobstructed freedom.

When Wonhyo Daesa began looking at the world through other people's perspectives instead of only his own, he realized the transient nature of the world. He realized that all things are created by the mind and that there was nothing that is dirty or clean. He discovered this after experiencing water tasting sweet when he didn't know he was drinking from a skull and immediately feeling nauseous once he discovered what he had done.

Even though he had learned from sutras that everything is created by the mind, and that nothing is inherently dirty or clean, he didn't really get it. Why? Because he vomited the water from the skull, believing it was dirty. At that moment, he realized that he actually didn't know. He was enlightened the moment he vomited. If he'd already been enlightened, there would have been no reason to vomit. His vomiting meant he was influenced by an external circumstance.

Lastly, he went from believing that a Mahayana bodhisattva should liberate sentient beings to realizing that there were no sentient beings outside of his mind. The *Diamond Sutra* says, "One should resolve to liberate all sentient beings, but after these beings have become liberated, in truth, you will know that not even a single being has been liberated because there is no such thing as a sentient being to begin with." This is what he realized.

Opportunities for awakening can be found in the midst of our lives, whenever we see and hear things, face difficulties, and argue about things being right or wrong. When we argue about things, we should know that we are the ones who are taking issue with them, but we rarely realize this. When we get angry, we should be aware that we're being affected by external circumstances, but we just aren't aware. That's why we can't be awakened.

If we live alone on a remote mountain, we'll have fewer chances to be awakened. As we live in the secular world, we have countless chances to be awakened, especially in a marital relationship. Our spouses know us like the back of their hand and can let us know when we've made any progress toward awakening. No one else can do that for us. When we brag, pretending that we've attained some awakening, they poke at our weak spots. At times like that, we have to realize that they're testing us. They say it is easier to be enlightened when we have a bad spouse. Having a partner is like having an excellent trainer. They've mastered the art of checking to see if we are awakened.

You have to practice in your daily lives. For example, suppose you're at stage one now, but you wish to move on to stage two. Therefore, you want to renounce the world and become a monk in order to advance to stage two and then return home and proceed to stage three and then to stage four. However, if you know that stage one and stage four are the same, there's no need to leave and return. As long as you're in the water, harvest pearls instead of floundering and shouting for help.

If you're married, have a child, are bankrupt, have cancer, or are old, instead of suffering, look for opportunities to be awakened. There are things you can realize only when you're old, sick, divorced, or have been stabbed in the back by someone you trust.

Wonhyo Daesa was awakened when he vomited the water he consumed after he discovered he drank it from a skull. Like Wonhyo Daesa, people experience situations that can awaken them multiple times a day. When asked why they aren't awakened, people say they haven't drunk water from a skull yet or that there are very few tombs around nowadays. They say if they knew where a tomb was, they would go there and experience what Wonhyo Daesa did.

This is the wrong way to think. Awakening is not far away. It can happen whenever the mind arises. Depending on whether or not you notice your mind has arisen, you could attain enlightenment all at once or go through the transmigration of life after life through the six realms of existence.

A Golden Opportunity

A female lay Buddhist I was acquainted with called me to say she had some good news. "Sunim, do you remember my wish? Well, my husband finally went with me to the temple."

This woman did a lot of volunteer work for the temple, but her husband had never joined her. In fact, he didn't accompany her anywhere even though it was common in their neighborhood for married couples to attend events together. This not only made her uncomfortable but also wounded her self-esteem. When only one member of a couple showed up at such events, people would begin to gossip about the couple. She told me that her temple had an end-of-the-year party for couples, and this time, her husband had accompanied her. Although she was happy her long cherished prayer had finally been answered, I gave her a warning, "A good thing is often accompanied by the bad. I hope you calm down and focus on practicing diligently. If you rejoice when things turn out the way you want, you will inevitably face disappointment. I'm not saying what happened is a bad thing. It's a good thing, but try not to be too excited about it."

The next day she called me again and said, "Sunim, I'm going to get a divorce." I congratulated her and told her that what happened to her that day was as good as what happened the day before.

Her husband was a doctor. She and her husband were both quite good-looking, and they both had good academic and family backgrounds. In their pride, they each thought their partner benefited more from their relationship. Even though they had married for love, they gradually allowed their pride to build walls around their hearts. Still, none of this showed on the surface.

The wife believed something improper was going on between her husband and a nurse at his office. However, every time she asked him about it, he denied it. She kept an eye on them but never found anything definitive. She continued to feel uneasy in her heart, but he continued to vehemently deny any wrongdoing. Their relationship grew increasingly more distant, and they avoided attending events together as much as possible.

When her husband accompanied her to the temple event, she initially felt exceedingly grateful. To show her gratitude, she decided to wash his clothes, something she'd never done before. While emptying his pockets, she found two movie tickets for a recent movie. The moment she saw them, she became furious. "Damn you," she thought, "you've thoroughly deceived me, but you can't get away with it this time. Now I have proof."

She immediately drove to her husband's office. She sent away the patient with whom he was consulting and demanded he tell her the truth. Her husband appeared shocked, but she urged him to admit he had lied to her and was having an affair with his nurse. Her proof was the movie tickets she waved in front of his face. She pressed him to admit that he'd gone to the movie with the nurse. Finally, her husband admitted, "All right. I did. What are you going to do about it?" She asked him how he could come home every day feeling unashamed, and eventually, he told her that he would do whatever she wanted him to do. "What do I want you to do? Let's get a divorce," she said. She would have refused to forgive him even if he'd begged her, but she was shocked by how easily he agreed to a divorce. Only a single day after being so happy about her husband accompanying her to an event, she was all set to divorce him.

After listening to her story, I said to her, "You missed such a golden opportunity. What a shame." What I meant was that she missed an opportunity for awakening. Before she saw the movie tickets, she was so happy with her husband, but after she saw them, she regarded him as her bitter enemy. Which was her true mind? Before seeing the tickets or after? It was the same as when Wonhyo Daesa drank the water from the skull. Before he knew the water was in a skull, it had tasted sweet, but after he knew, he vomited even though he knew the water was the same. The moment he believed the water was dirty and vomited, he gained enlightenment.

The woman's fury was not in the movie tickets; it was in the mind. Huineung, the sixth patriarch, said, "What was your mind before, and what is your mind now? Which is your true self?" Opportunities like this occur several times a day. But we lose those opportunities because we're wandering around looking for Wonhyo Daesa's skull. We mistakenly believe we cannot become awakened because we don't have an opportunity to drink water out of a skull.

The Moment Love Turns into Hate

There is a saying that you come to hate someone because you love them. One of my acquaintances exemplified this.

This man was so totally in love with his wife that he thought about her constantly even at work, calling her several times a day just so he could hear her voice. One afternoon, he had to run an errand, but he finished sooner than he expected. So, he decided to drop by his house to see his wife. He did not call ahead of time because he wanted to surprise her, but when he entered the house, he found his wife sitting with another man. He went totally crazy and divorced her.

The man sitting with his wife might have been her friend

or might have been there on business, but someone as obsessive as this man was incapable of listening to reason. Convinced that he'd been betrayed, he simply went crazy the moment he saw the stranger in the house with his wife. But a moment like this one can be a good opportunity for awakening. You come home to spend time with your wife because you miss her, but after seeing her with another man, you go out of your mind with jealousy. That moment is the same as the one when Wonhyo Daesa vomited after he realized he'd drunk water from a skull. Awakening occurs at such moments.

You probably have had many opportunities like that one. Be aware that such a moment is a golden opportunity to attain enlightenment. Don't let it pass you by. Whether or not your husband went to a movie with another woman or had an affair isn't important. After attaining enlightenment, drinking water from a skull is no longer important. These moments happen many times a day. When you turn your eyes inward and really look at yourself, you can see such contradictions. If you keep looking outward, you will miss them.

Getting a bad result after doing something with a good

intention is the same. After listening to a Dharma talk, you decide to do something nice for your husband. Without telling him, you prepare a delicious meal and even buy an expensive bottle of liquor. You set a beautiful table as you look forward to telling him, "Honey, I'm sorry I haven't been very nice to you lately. I know you've been having a hard time at work." But then he doesn't come home at dinner time. You wait an hour and "honey" changes to "jerk." Three hours pass and you get angrier and angrier. If you hadn't made such a big deal of this dinner, you wouldn't have cared whether he came home late. He, on the other hand, doesn't know anything about your plans. When he comes home, you're seething. However, having listened to the Dharma talk that day, you suppress your anger and serve dinner. That's when he tells you he's already eaten and asks why you waited so long to eat yours. And at that point, you explode.

Good intentions don't always produce a good result. Good intentions as well as bad ones can produce bad results. Sometimes, good intentions produce a worse result because our unfulfilled expectations make us angry. Like the above example, our lives are filled with countless opportunities to awaken.

If you observe yourself a little, you'll see that two contradictory things often arise in your mind at the same time. When your attention is turned inward, you will be aware of this, but if your attention is turned outward, you won't see it. That's when people say they have to hate, leave, or kill a person because of how much they love them. If you turn your eyes inward, you'll see the contradiction. Continue to look outward, and you won't notice it. If you love someone, you have reasons to love them. If you hate someone, you have reasons to hate them. The wife will think trying to be good to her husband because she loves him was a good thing, but she also can't help hating him because, not knowing her intention, he came home late. At that point, the husband thinks his wife is crazy because she was smiling one minute and furious the next. We often find ourselves being contradictory in this way.

What I'm saying is that we shouldn't be deceived by ourselves. Many supposedly good things turn out to be bad later on. We need to carefully examine our lives. Awakening exists in our everyday lives. Great Seon masters in the past did not necessarily attain enlightenment while practicing in the mountains. When you look directly at the contradiction in your mind, the way to awakening opens up. Therefore, don't look outside. Look inside.

PART 06

BE AWAKE TO THE HERE AND NOW

We always forget our current role. Some try to teach when they are there to learn. Others neglect their duties when they are there to teach. And still others badmouth the people to whom they should be grateful for the help they received. We won't have any regrets in our lives if we are awake to these three things: Now, here, and why. We regret later because we are not awake now.

Be a Pine Tree in Front of the Pagoda

When I was young, I constantly complained about the established practice of Buddhism. I thought Buddhism and the monks who practiced it needed to be reformed, and I devoted myself to the Buddhist reform movement. I was even willing to sacrifice my life in order to bring about these changes. One day, while I was talking to my Dharma teacher about the many problems that existed in the way Buddhism was being practiced, he told me, "Be a pine tree in front of the pagoda."

He meant that, when it is young, the tree initially resents the pagoda because it is obstructed from view by the pagoda.

But the tree shouldn't be resentful because when it grows to maturity, it will obstruct the pagoda from view. He was telling me that I shouldn't blame or complain about others and that I should focus on doing the right thing myself.

While traveling in America, I found myself once again criticizing and complaining about the established practice of Buddhism to an elderly monk I had just met. The elderly monk listened patiently to everything I had to say. After I went on and on for two hours, he told me,

"Young man,
when a person sits on a ridge between rice paddies
and keeps one's mind pure,
that person is a practitioner.
And the place where that person sits is a temple.
That is Buddhism."

His words shocked me to the core. I believed a monk was someone who shaved his head and wore a robe. It never occurred to me that any person with a pure mind was a monk. I thought a temple had to be a building with a tile roof, never thinking a temple was simply the place where a practitioner stays. What did this have to do with me? I had complained that Buddhism needed to be reformed, but I defined a monk as a person with a shaved head and a temple as a building with a tiled roof. Everything that I had been doing was an exercise in futility because what I'd been trying to reform was not actually Buddhism. It was as if I'd been trying to pluck an illusory flower from the air. Trying to grasp a flower where none exists is a pointless act no matter how hard you try. My efforts were doomed to fail because I was trying to reform something that was not Buddhism. In plain language, the monk told me that I was deluded and that my efforts were totally futile. An experience like this is an awakening.

Holding onto Myself

I once worked for a season as a menial worker for Bongamsa Temple in Mungyeong, South Korea. My true identity was known only to the temple's Seon master, Seoam Sunim. He asked me why I wanted to work as a menial worker when I was already busy spreading the Buddha's teachings. I told him I wanted to live quietly as a menial worker just for that season and asked him to pretend that he didn't know me.

I lived at the temple, cutting wood, weeding fields, cleaning the privies, and doing farm work. One day, a beggar showed up, and I noticed that he didn't have a physical disability and his clothes were decent. We talked for a while, and I suggested he work with me because the temple was short of workers. I led him to a nearby stream, so he could wash himself, gave him new clothes, and invited him to share my small room.

Even though the morning chanting was held at 3 o'clock in the morning, I participated in it every morning, labored all day, and then participated in the evening chanting. The newcomer thought I was just another menial worker until he noticed that I participated in the morning and evening chanting. One day, he asked me if I was a monk. I denied it but inquired why he thought I might be. He then asked why I participated in the morning chanting if I wasn't a monk.

I thought that what I was doing was the right thing. I thought hiding my identity and working as a menial worker was a good thing and that participating in the morning chanting was also good. However, my ruse had been discovered. This man, who knew nothing about me, already suspected my true identity because he found my behavior as a menial worker odd. Even though I had gone to great lengths to have the outward appearance of a laborer, some of my actions gave away my true identity. Maybe that's why they say that you can fool a ghost but not a man.

Attending the morning chanting wasn't the only thing that revealed who I was. I paid extra attention when changing the coal briquettes that heated the rooms housing the elderly monks. About a month into my stay, an elderly monk called me over. He nudged me in the ribs and asked, "You're hiding from the police because you participated in demonstrations, aren't you?"

Once again, I was exposed. A real menial worker would have occasionally been lazy and let the fire die out. My behavior was seen as strange for a menial worker. I was hard-working and meticulous, so I wasn't acting like a typical worker. I had hidden my appearance as a monk behind the attire of a menial worker but was unable to be anyone but myself. When I let go of myself, I should have had no self, but I couldn't seem to completely let go of who I was.

One day, while I was sitting in the Buddha Hall for the evening service, some postulants were pouring fresh water in the water bowl and emptying the incense burner, but they couldn't remember where the water bowl and incense burner should be placed. As they were arguing among themselves about it, I interrupted them and told them where they should be placed. That made them angry. "What do you know about it to butt in like that?" Those postulants had just joined the temple, and they were still timid and nervous in the presence of senior monks. But in front of lay Buddhists, they acted like they owned the temple. I became furious as they scolded me.

However, the moment my anger rose, I saw myself and recognized that to the postulants I was just a lay Buddhist. Such moments offer you an opportunity to truly see yourself. In my case, I realized that I was still holding onto my identity as a monk even though I thought I'd let go of myself simply because I had changed my clothes.

I worked really hard as a menial worker, but I hadn't gone there to work hard. I was there to let go of my obsession about work, whether good or bad. I was there to reflect on myself. Instead of changing my habit of working hard, I simply replaced the work of spreading the Dharma with wood cutting and the recitation of Buddhist chants with weeding. Karma – in other words, habits – is hard to change. That is why karma is so scary.

One day, as I was sweating profusely while vigorously chopping wood, I lifted my head and saw the temple's Seon Master watching me. As I bowed to him, he said, "Young man, Bongamsa Temple was doing fine even before you came." I realized that I was working frantically as if the temple couldn't run without me. But Bongamsa Temple had been doing fine before I showed up. The Seon Master was telling me that I was too attached to work and that I needed to let go of that attachment.

Are You Awake?

I spent some time reflecting on why I was working so hard, trying to discover what I was attached to. I came to realize that I was guarding myself against criticism. Since I was unable to let go of myself, I worked frantically to avoid being criticized once my identity was revealed. I didn't want anyone saying, "When he was a menial worker at the temple, he shirked his responsibilities. He was a worthless fellow." This is how we hold onto ourselves. Even when we're pursuing a goal, we often become attached to the process, try to justify what we're doing, and end up failing to achieve the goal. In the end, my lifestyle remained the same no matter where I was.

I didn't go to Bongamsa Temple to perform tasks or make changes. As the Seon master said, Bongsamsa Temple was doing just fine before I arrived. I was there to change myself, but instead, I acted like I was there to change the temple. Because I had identified some problems in the temple while staying there, I was determined to correct them.

Long ago, there was a Seon master who often called his own name and asked a question, and then he answered himself. You should try doing that yourself. You ask, "So and so, why did you come here? What did you come here for?" You answer, "I came here as a postulant." Then, you ask again, "Well then, are you doing well as a postulant?"

There are many individuals who act like teachers even though they are at the temple as postulants. Or they act like senior monks even though they are at the temple as lay Buddhists. How difficult must life be for these people due to such disparities? People are able to see all the contradictions in those they live with, but they are blind to their own. You have to ask yourself, "Why am I here? What am I here to do?" and then decide if your behavior matches the purpose. That is being awake in the present moment.

However, we always forget our responsibilities. There are

A Taste of Enlightenment

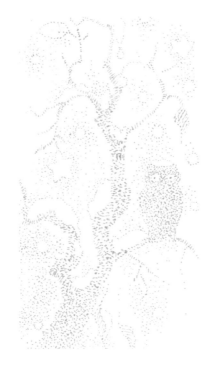

Young man,
when a person sits on a ridge between rice paddies
and keeps one's mind pure,
that person is a practitioner.
And the place where that person sits is a temple.
That is Buddhism.

people who came to learn but instead try to teach; there are people who came to teach but don't; and there are people who should be thankful for the help they receive but instead criticize those who help them. If we are awake to these three things — here, now, and why — there won't be any need for regret in our lives. We have regrets later because we are not awake now.

Therefore, call your name like the Seon master from long ago. Call your name and then ask, "Are you awake?" Always check on yourself so that you can answer, "Yes, I am."

United We Fall,
Divided We Stand

While I was at Bongamsa Temple, I learned a lot from the coworker who had been a beggar. He was the one who said, "United we fall, divided we stand."

At first, I couldn't understand what that meant. I asked him why he had reversed the saying, adding that the correct version was "United we stand, divided we fall." He insisted his version was the right one. He explained that when beggars are with other beggars, they often drink a lot. As a result, countless beggars end up dying from alcohol addiction, many before age forty. To avoid this, they needed to separate themselves from each other – in other words, divide themselves. He said that he had almost died because of his alcohol addiction, so he chose to leave his fellow beggars.

It seemed like a plausible story. There are real-life examples to which this modified saying applies. Some married couples continuously wage war against each other. Such couples are better off separated. Divorce is better for them. For me, this was a new way of looking at things.

One day each fortnight, the members of the temple worked on various tasks that needed to be done around the temple. As the monks weeded the fields and carried water, lay Buddhists would express their concern, telling the monks that they were working too hard and that they should stop and rest. My coworker said to me, "What strange people these lay Buddhists are." When I asked why, he answered, "These people say nothing when they see us working every day, so why are they making such a fuss over monks who work for such a short time?"

His words surprised me. This was such a different perspective on monks. Then, he added, "I used to wonder what monks do, but I finally figured it out." "What do they do?" I asked. "They just eat and poop," he answered. I asked how he came to that conclusion. He told me that as far as he could tell, the monks would go into the meditation room after their meals and stay there until they had to go to the restroom. And once done, they would go back into the meditation room to repeat the process again. To him, it seemed like they produced poop without accomplishing much else. This was a keen observation. We attach meaning to the monks' actions, stating that they are meditating or practicing, but in his eyes, it was simply a process for turning rice into poop.

When we worked to empty out all the urine and feces from the toilet, I would fill my container about 80% full and carry it very carefully, whereas my coworker would fill his about a third full and carry it very easily. I nagged him about this during our break: "Even though we're just hired hands, we need to work hard. How can you fill your container only a third full?"

His reply was, "You don't know anything about working as a manual laborer."

"What do you mean?"

"As a manual laborer, our body is the only thing we have. If we get hurt, it's like losing all our possessions. We need to keep our body healthy all the time."

I said, "Even so, we should work hard, take a break, work hard again, and take another break. What you're doing isn't right."

"Jeez, you really know nothing about manual labor. If you work hard, finish your work early and take a rest, your employer won't like it. They'll hate seeing you take a break. They'll be happier if you continuously work little by little without taking a rest."

At first, I couldn't understand his reasoning. But once I gave it some thought, I realized he was right. A master hates to see their servant resting. A business owner hates to see their employees take a break. My coworker's words contained a lot of wisdom.

But I didn't follow his advice and, unlike a typical manual laborer, continued working hard. Eventually, I became ill. My body broke down because I pushed it past its capacity while I continued to attend morning and evening chanting. After about a month and a half, I found myself totally exhausted. My throat was so sore I couldn't swallow my own saliva.

When I could no longer stand the pain, I went to a pharmacy in town for some medicine. My coworker told me

A Taste of Enlightenment

that a senior monk had visited while I was out. Somehow, he knew I was sick and had left some honey for me. My coworker already had his suspicions about my identity, but when the senior monk brought me honey, the coworker knew I wasn't a typical menial worker. The next morning, he was gone. Maybe he was worried he would get in trouble because he had badmouthed the monks freely with me. We'd promised to leave the temple together as beggars, but he left without me.

I learned a lot from that fellow. I would have learned even more if I hadn't been so set in my ways that my identity was revealed. This occurred because I was only able to change my appearance but not my inner self. As a result, I was only able to fool those around me for a short time.

When you practice, you have opportunities to learn wherever you are. You can learn when you fall down on the street, you can learn when you quarrel with someone, you can learn from a mistake, and you can learn from a failure. You just need to have the wisdom to harvest pearls if you happen to fall into the sea.

When parents are raising their children, they tell them to behave in a certain way, but children seldom do as they are told. Similarly, children make suggestions to their parents, but parents seldom change their behavior. It's not that they don't acknowledge their children's suggestions. They say they'll follow their advice, but in the end, they simply continue to do things their own way. At times like this, children wonder why their parents can't change, and they become resentful.

There is a reason for this. Just like there are reasons for the rain that falls during the rainy season and just like there are reasons for a dam to fail, there is a reason why people behave that way.

Then, what is the reason? The reason people continue to do things their way is because, at the moment they're doing it, they believe what they are doing is right. Afterwards, they might regret their actions and decide they were wrong or foolish, but at the moment of the action, they're sure they're doing the right thing. No one consciously chooses to take the wrong path. At the moment a person commits suicide, they kill themselves because they believe it's a better option than staying alive. A person who kills someone else also does so because they think it's the right choice at that moment.

When you're angry and someone wonders how a disciple of the Buddha can get angry, what do you tell them? You're not likely to acknowledge right away that a disciple of the Buddha shouldn't get angry. Instead, you'll respond that it's only natural for a person to get angry in the situation you found yourself in, that you're not a Buddha, and that the situation would have made anyone angry. When people claim they aren't a Buddha, the underlying meaning is that they'd rather choose to get angry over becoming a Buddha. We get angry because we think it's the better choice even though avoiding anger is the way to become a Buddha.

A person who does something that seems not only wrong but ridiculous to you actually does it because from their perspective it's right and makes perfect sense. If someone thinks something is right, and you think it's wrong, this is just a matter of differing points of view. The results are all due to different karmas, habits, and thought patterns. That is why, once we reach enlightenment, we can see that everything is truth. We cannot objectively decide whether something is right or wrong. Even though something seems wrong to you, the person who does it believes it's right. They might continue to think they were right, or they may realize later that the action was wrong and regret it. But at the moment they do something, they do it because they think they're right. To solve life's problems, you have to accept this reality. Whether it's good or bad, this is the way people think, behave, and live.

No Reason to Blame Others

Since this is the way people live, everyone harbors resentment in their heart. When we think we've been unfairly criticized because, in our own view, we believe we acted correctly, all of us feel resentment or anger. We feel bitter toward the world, our husbands, our parents, our children, fellow monks, or lay Buddhists because we don't get the results we want despite our best efforts, and because we get criticized. Succumbing to the forces of money, power, or an authority figure, we decide to do as we are told. Yet, when faced with a similar situation, we revert to our previous behavior pattern.

A husband cheats on his wife and begs her forgiveness,

swearing he'll never do it again. He even tells her that she can divorce him if he does it again. A gambler swears they will cut off their hand if they gamble again. A borrower swears they will never ask for money again if, just this once, you lend them money. Yet, if a similar situation arises, they all behave in exactly the same way as before.

Others may wonder why these people can't change their behavior, but when they face a similar situation, the thoughts that made them behave that way arise again. This is not a conscious decision on their part. It's simply the way their mind works at the moment they act. In Buddhist terms, this is called karma.

Originally, karma was not a Buddhist term but an Indian one. In Buddhism, the volitional formations among five aggregates, known as sankhara (the predilections, biases, likes and dislikes, and other attributes that make up our psychological profile) are close to the meaning of karma. In today's terms, we refer to this as habit or subconsciousness. The mind arises from it, and actions follow right after.

The actions we take based on the belief we are doing the right thing often lead to undesired results. So, we suffer. Our current lives are the result of the choices we have made for ourselves. In our own way, we've done the best we could. When we lie down, sit down, eat something, or don't listen to others, we perform these actions thinking they are our best course of action at the time. That's why it's said that we are the ones deciding our fate, not others. For example, we lie, not because we want to lie, but because in the moment we lie, we believe lying is better than telling the truth.

We think, "If I tell the truth, it will only complicate matters, so I'll avoid the whole problem by lying." Sometimes, we lie for our own sake, but sometimes we lie for others. We act, thinking we're doing the right thing the moment we are doing it. As we live our lives believing we are doing right, we should be happy. But are we? If we haven't gotten the result we wanted, we need to investigate what went wrong.

We blame others for the unintended results of our actions. We insist the unwanted outcome is due to our husband, wife, parent, child, or boss. If that doesn't solve the problem, we go on to beg the Buddha, God, the Mountain God, Dragon King, or whomever we consider more powerful than ourselves, to solve the problem. When none of this works, we become fatalistic, believing we can't escape God's will no matter what we do. So, we pray to the gods for dear life. In India, people blame it on karma from a previous life, so they go to ascetics, those who practice a very austere lifestyle, to find out about their previous life. In China, they blame it on the time of their birth, so they spend their time trying to find out what the time of their birth signifies. All this happens because we all spend our time looking in the wrong places for the cause of our suffering, that is, outside of ourselves.

But when you analyze your problems one at a time, you'll discover that they all originate from inside you. Depending on what type of seeds are planted, after it rains, a pumpkin, melon, or a sesame shoot will sprout. Even though the seed sprouts after the field is watered, the field and the water are only external conditions and not the fundamental causes of the sprouting. If a seed contains the genetic components of a pumpkin, a pumpkin shoot will sprout. The same is true for a melon or a sesame plant seed. You can blame an unwanted outcome on your husband, child, or friend, but the truth is that things turn out the way they do because you already carry inside you the seed that will germinate in such a way.

On the other hand, if a seed isn't planted, it won't sprout. Since a seed only sprouts when it's planted in soil, it may

A Taste of Enlightenment

seem that the field is the cause. This is a delusion. This is the error in perception described in the *Heart Sutra*. That's why the Buddha teaches us to turn our attention inward instead of outward and to observe our inner self more deeply.

PART 07

TURN THINGS THAT
HAVE ALREADY HAPPENED INTO
SOMETHING USEFUL IN YOUR LIFE

All things that happen are neither good nor bad. What you consider good today could turn into something bad tomorrow. What you consider bad today could turn into something good tomorrow. They say falling down is bad, but if you find some money on the ground when you fall, then falling down becomes a good thing. Everything is just an incident. It's up to you to make it into something useful in your life.

The Pain of Death and
Abstaining from Killing

One morning a long time ago, some strangers barged into my house without warning, blindfolded me, and dragged me to an unknown location. There, without warning, they started to beat me as they tried to force me to confess to some crime. As they tortured me, they said I was more stubborn than a North Korean spy. They beat my feet with a baseball bat, pressed against my back until it felt like my spine would snap, and waterboarded me. I struggled and screamed for my life. I kept hoping I would pass out, but it never happened, so I kept answering their questions with the first things that came to my mind. Since I didn't know anything, there was no way my answers could be right. When they checked and found my answers were wrong, they tortured me again. This process was repeated several times.

Once, while I was screaming in pain, I reached a point where I almost fainted. It was at that point that an image appeared in my head like it would on a screen in a movie theater, an image of a trembling, dying frog. I can't tell you how indescribably shocking this image was to me.

This image was of a frog that I had killed when I was a boy. I lived in a rural area throughout elementary school. I would often walk along the ridge between rice paddies looking for frogs. When I spotted one, I would whack its spine with a branch from a clover bush and watch as the frog sprawled out, trembled, and died. I killed a lot of frogs. I cut up the larger ones and fed the torso to the chickens while I ate the legs. I wasn't the only one doing this; it was a common practice for children in rural areas. I had forgotten all about this until it flashed in my mind while I was being tortured. I realized I was just like that frog. Just like when I whacked its spine, my back was being stretched over a threshold while being pushed down from above. My back hurt so badly that I trembled uncontrollably, just like the dying frog from my childhood.

My detention and torture occurred after I had been a Buddhist for ten years. I was confident in my knowledge of Buddhism and had some experience leading Buddhist movements and teaching Buddhist doctrines to young people. Still, I'd always harbored doubts about the precept of abstaining from killing living beings. I had immediately understood other precepts, such as abstaining from stealing, sexual misconduct, telling lies, and consuming intoxicants. My thought was that living involved killing, so how could we survive without killing? We kill animals so we can eat. In a war, we kill our enemies. Even Samyeong Daesa, a leading warrior monk during the Japanese invasion of Korea from 1592 to 1598, killed Japanese soldiers when Japan invaded Korea. I thought this precept made Buddhism a bit passive. Since Buddhism prohibits killing under any circumstances, I thought this would make it difficult to take an active position in attacking the opposition while sacrificing ourselves for social justice. I could have understood it more easily if the precept was just against killing people. But as the precept prohibits the killing of even the tiniest creature, my mind always harbored doubts about it.

I didn't think it was wrong when I killed the frogs. Since I needed to eat to survive, I thought it was only natural to do this and that it wasn't a grave sin. However, when I found myself in the frog's position, I could no longer deny it was wrong. From that point on, I could no longer say it was all right to torture and beat someone if they did something wrong. Even though I'd been a practicing Buddhist for ten years and taught Buddhism to others, I did not wholly accept the Buddha's teachings, entertaining doubts if they differed from my own opinions. Only after being put in the frog's position did I realize that abstaining from killing was a precept I needed to accept unconditionally.

How blind had I been to view the Buddha's teachings through my own personal filter, even questioning his teachings if they didn't suit me? Only once it became personal for me did I recognize my own foolishness. While I claimed to be a Buddhist, I didn't even accept the Buddha's first precept, the abstinence from killing all living beings. When I killed, I said it couldn't be helped, but when I was put in a position where I could be killed, I was furious, resentful, and horrified.

The image of the frog made me realize that someone like me deserved to die. I had spent ten years studying the Buddha's teachings but still hadn't accepted them. How was I able to become awakened? People struggle tenaciously when they want to live, but when they decide they deserve to die, they stop. They just shut down. That's what happened to me. I no longer felt pain and could barely process being tortured. I became oblivious to my surroundings and my body went limp. Then, the torture stopped. When I stopped struggling and accepted death, the torture came to an end. This experience was a great awakening for me. I realized that I had not really accepted the knowledge I thought I'd gained through studying Buddhism. The ability to use Buddhist terminology didn't mean I knew Buddhism. It just meant that I interpreted the scriptures as they suited me.

During my stay in prison, indescribable thoughts arose in my head while I gazed through the restroom window at the lights from distant apartments. I imagined families or friends having pleasant conversations in those apartments. None of them would be aware of the suffering I was experiencing somewhere so close to them. Some of them might even be talking about Buddhism, a bodhisattva's way of life, enlightenment, or the liberation of sentient beings. They would be enjoying their idle ideological arguments, totally unaware that I was desperately begging for help in the face of death.

Until my imprisonment, I wasn't any different. Until it happened to me, it never occurred to me that someone like me could be arrested. When I saw someone else being taken to the police station, I thought they must have committed a crime and that no one would be taken into custody unless they had done something wrong. I believed that being dragged to a police station would never happen to someone who didn't commit a crime. When I found myself wrongfully imprisoned and being tortured, I learned that sometimes you can be subject to persecution even though you haven't done anything wrong. Previously, I thought that even though torturing prisoners was socially condoned, I could avoid being tortured. However, I came to realize that as long as torture existed in the world, anyone, including me, could be subject to torture. Therefore, my view changed from being careful in order to avoid torture to making the world free from torture altogether.

Until that point, I didn't understand why the bodhi-sattvas aspired to build Jungto. Creating a world without

---

Jungto is a land where individuals are happy, society is peaceful, and nature is beautiful.

A Taste of Enlightenment

gender inequality, prejudice against physical disability, social discrimination, hunger, disease, and war is not just for other people's benefits; it is actually for *my* benefit. This experience provided me with the opportunity to view the world as it is, realize the greatness of the Buddha, and wholly accept all of the Buddha's teachings.

After that, when I came across a part of the Buddha's teachings or a sutra that I did not understand or could not fully accept, I didn't judge those parts as inaccurate or wrong. Instead, I skipped them for the time being, considering them an area I did not yet understand.

Things you realize through experience exist on a totally different level from things you learn through books or from someone else's words. There is a big difference between a realization that hits you instantaneously due to something you've experienced, and one you understand theoretically through repeated listening and reading. After my experience of being falsely imprisoned, I began to carry out social movements based on my experiences rather than on the theories I had learned.

True Understanding

As I was tortured, I felt both extreme pain and extreme rage. I was boiling with rage because I was being tortured for no reason. I thought to myself, "When I get out, I'll kill all of you." If my hand had been a gun, I would have shot them right away. I was in so much rage I couldn't see straight. The only reason I didn't kill them was because I lacked the means.

Those who are tortured struggle with all their strength, so three big men are needed to carry out the torture. Of course, the person being tortured suffers great physical pain, but it is also physically taxing for the torturers, so they need to take occasional breaks from their work.

During one of those breaks, while smoking cigarettes, one of my torturers said, "Today, my daughter is taking the college entrance exam. I am worried that she might not do well. I want her to be admitted into a college in Seoul. If she has to go to a college in a remote city, it will be financially difficult for us." The men exchanged comments and continued the conversation on the subject. They were talking about the same things people discuss in an ordinary tavern.

Until that point, I had viewed them as evil. I came to realize that when they went home, they were loving husbands to their wives, loving fathers to their children, and loving sons to their parents – that is, ordinary people. They were hard working, model government employees. They were ordinary people whose wives might thank them for their hard work and prepare dinner for them when they get home from work. Their children might talk to them about their day or the exams they had taken. They weren't my enemies although until that moment, I wondered how humans could torture another human being like that.

Upon this realization, all the hatred I felt toward them, a rage potent enough to make me want to kill ten or twenty of them, disappeared. I came to understand that each of them was simply another human being. I could finally understand the parts I had found difficult to comprehend while reading the Bible or Buddhist sutras. It was very difficult for me to accept the statement, "Do not try to prove your innocence when you are falsely accused," in *Bowangsammaeron.* And I hadn't been able to accept what Jesus said when he was dying on the cross, "Father, forgive them, for they know not what they do." Through my experience, I was able to both understand what this meant and accept it. The executioners were just doing their job. Jesus understood them perfectly, so he wasn't angry but forgave them, instead of wanting to punish them.

All the work I am involved in today is based on this experience. Many South Koreans say that the North Koreans are bad, but when you actually listen to what North Koreans have to say, you discover that, in their own way, they are doing what they believe to be right. Americans are criticized by many, but when you listen to Americans, they also think they're doing right in their own way. The Japanese say North

---

Bowangsammaeron is the ancient Buddhist teachings of a monk, which describes how practitioners should behave in their daily life.

Koreans are like devils. They gnash their teeth in anger, asking how North Koreans can kidnap people in broad daylight. They dislike North Koreans more than Koreans dislike the Japanese. North Korea is quite a hot topic in Japan right now. However, if you let North Koreans know this, they get absolutely furious. They don't think the Japanese have the right to talk that way about them when the Japanese haven't apologized to or compensated the 200,000 women they shipped to Manchuria, the Philippines, and Indonesia as comfort women; the tens of thousands of students they used as cannon fodder; and the more than one million people they used as forced labor during the Japanese Colonial Era.

When I travel to India, Indians say the Pakistanis are bad, and when I meet Pakistanis, they say the same about Indians. Palestinians say Israelis are bad, and Israelis say Palestinians are bad. It seems as if there are only victims in this world and no perpetrators.

Photographs of people who died and the damage caused by the nuclear bombs are displayed at Peace Park in Hiroshima. We think of the Japanese as the perpetrators, don't we? But those who work for the peace movement in Japan believe Japan was the victim. On the other hand, there is a museum in Changchun, China that exhibits the brutality of the medical experiments perpetrated on the Chinese by the Japanese. It's disturbing to view the harrowing images of the victims who suffered so horribly.

So, how can we ever achieve reconciliation? The so-called right-wing conservatives in South Korea talk about families who were killed and properties that were confiscated by the Communists in Korea after the end of the Japanese colonial rule. However, there have been many cases of the Korean army and police force massacring entire villages under the name of eradicating communism. One example is the Bodo League, a massacre and war crime against communists and suspected sympathizers that occurred in the summer of 1950 during the Korean War. In some villages, many families hold a memorial service for their ancestors on the same day. Many people were killed on Jeju Island during the April 3rd uprising, an attempted insurgency that was followed by an anti-communist suppression campaign. If you visit North Korea and listen to the people, they say Americans bombed and burned to the ground whole villages without leaving a single house standing. Their hatred toward imperialist America, their sworn enemy, is beyond words. But in South

Korea, some people will read you the riot act if you try to bad-mouth America. All these people live under the same sky.

When you listen to a wife complain about her husband, you wonder how the husband could act in the way she describes. When you listen to a story about a husband having affairs, squandering the family fortune, or beating his wife, you wonder why he bothered to marry in the first place. Then, when you hear the husband's side of the story, you wonder how any woman could be so vicious. If you want to live peacefully in such situations, you have to understand the other person's position.

If I ask a wife to try to understand her husband's position when she complains that her life is unhappy because of him, she accuses me of taking his side because I'm a man. When a husband complains that his life is unhappy because of his wife, I tell him to try to understand his wife's position. Then, he complains that I'm just saying that because I've never been married. It's the same when I explain North Korea's position to the U.S., the U.S.'s position to North Korea, North Korea's position to South Korea, and South Korea's position to North Korea. To resolve a problem step by step, you have to begin by recognizing the other's position, and seeing things from their perspective. This is what the Buddha taught. After reading sutras and listening to Dharma talks countless times, you start to believe you understand others, but you only truly come to understand someone by actually walking in their shoes.

When you're raising your own child, you begin to understand how hard it was for your parents to bring you into the world and raise you. Until then, no matter how often your parents tried to tell you, you wouldn't listen. Sometimes, frustrated parents go as far as to say, "You'll never understand until you raise a child as troublesome as you." If you think about it, it's almost a curse. When you hear this, you feel confident that things won't turn out that way. You declare that you won't live like your mother. However, when you're raising your own child who turns out to be quite troublesome, you end up admitting, "Heavens, I guess this is the reality of life."

After experiencing all kinds of things in life, I was able to see that there wasn't much difference in the relationships between couples, parents and children, friends, North Korea and South Korea, North Korea and the U.S., and the majority and minority parties. All problems arise from a self-centered perspective. People argue, feel resentful, and suffer because they look at the world only from their own perspectives. In other words, people's insistence on their own ways is driving these problems. If you let go of it, there's nothing in the world to fight about. You come to see that people are naturally different and that these differences can enrich the world in harmony.

The first time I realized this was when I was being tortured. From my perspective as a victim, my torturers were indescribably evil. However, when I listened to their conversation, I realized that they were ordinary men making a living. They were regular people who worried about their children, their families, and making ends meet on their meager salaries. In this sense, awakening transcends theory. It's not something you come to know by putting your brain to work. Ultimately, it is the interdependence of all things. It's the ability to see both sides instead of only one. When you can do that, all the contradictions are resolved. When you only look at a single side, you end up saying, "For me to live, you must die." But when you look at both sides, a way opens up which makes it possible for both you and the other person to live.

The World as It Is

The Buddha's teachings often seem complex and sophisticated, but once you see the truth, you'll realize how they are directly connected to the suffering you are experiencing right now. There is no need for sophisticated language.

Arguing who's right or wrong is form. People spend a lot of time arguing about right and wrong. When you listen to the daughter-in-law's story, she seems to be right, and when you listen to her mother-in-law's story, so does she. This is form. Once you hear both sides of the story, you can see that their opinions are simply different, and there's nothing that is right or wrong about either story. This is emptiness.

People on the west side of a mountain call it East Mountain, and those on its east side call it West Mountain. This is form. However, to those looking from a different side, it is neither East Mountain nor West Mountain. That is emptiness. Therefore, form is emptiness, and emptiness is form. Form does not differ from emptiness, and emptiness does not differ from form. According to the *Diamond Sutra*, "Form is not form," which means it is emptiness. People often insist that something is right or wrong, but there is nothing that can be determined to be right or wrong. All these judgments arise in the mind. In other words, everything is created by the mind.

When something occurs, we often say it's lucky and good, or it's unlucky and bad. The truth is that there is no good or bad incident. An incident is just an incident. An incident that is good or bad, lucky or unlucky, belongs to the world of phenomena. However, in the world of truth, how people interpret an incident makes it either a blessing or a disaster.

People sometimes say their husband is a bad person or their wife is a bad person, but, in fact, no one is a bad person. Every person is simply a person. You consider him

You can see that
their opinions are simply different,
and it's impossible to tell
who is right and who is wrong.
This is emptiness.

or her to be good or bad, but he or she is just a person. This is the concept of emptiness again. If you believe the other person to be bad, you suffer. If you believe the other person to be good, you're happy. Such beliefs and thoughts that arise in people's minds are form. So, if we're going to raise such thoughts in our minds, it's better for us to have positive thoughts.

All the Buddhist doctrines and the Buddha's teachings are very simple. When I say that form is emptiness, and emptiness is form, or that all forms are unreal, people think I'm talking about some deep and profound philosophy. But when I use everyday terms to explain these same concepts, they think I'm talking about trivialities because I use stories from everyday life. However, in both cases, I'm talking about the same thing. Even though I talk about the everyday problems in life, at their base lies the Buddhist view of the world. You don't have to read Buddhist sutras to understand the Buddhist view of the world. The true nature of the world we experience every day is the Buddhist view of the world. This is the true nature of all things, which means "all things as they are."

But do we view the world as it is? No. We look at the

world upside down. This is called delusion and is caused by an error in our perception. It means that people see illusions and are caught up in delusions, so everything is like a dream or a mirage. When you see that all forms are illusive and unreal, you'll begin to perceive your true Buddha-nature. In other words, if you know that all forms are unreal, you will perceive your true Buddha-nature. We may denounce someone as a rascal, condemn someone as evil, or declare them as our enemies. But these are all forms we create, get caught up in, and cling to.

We have to thoughtfully examine our lives. Getting tortured is a bad thing, but if you are awakened during the process, it's a good thing, a fortunate thing. This doesn't mean I would want to be tortured again or that I had to be tortured because it was a fortunate event for me. It would have been betther if it hadn't happened, but it did, and it didn't turn out to be a complete loss. If I had not been tortured but had stayed in my comfortable life, how could I have experienced such a profound awakening? So, it wasn't a good thing or a bad thing. If I learn a lesson from it, it will be a good thing for me. If I harbor a grudge and suffer because of it, it will be a misfortune in my life.

Things that happen in life are neither good nor bad in themselves. Things you currently consider to be good could become bad tomorrow, and things you consider bad could become good tomorrow. Things are just things. It's entirely up to you to make them useful to you.

The Present Is the Sum of
Past Causes and Conditions

We tend to blame others for the things that go wrong in our lives. But your current situation has been created by you and not by anyone else, not even the tiniest bit. Your present situation is the result of the choices you made at each step of the way as you decided one choice was better than another.

Let's say you are confronted by a mugger on the street. They hold a knife to your throat and threaten to kill you unless you give them your money. You'd probably choose to continue to live and give them your money or even your wedding ring, no matter how precious it is to you. If they threaten to kill you unless you have sex with them, you have no choice but to comply even if you are the most chaste woman in the world. You might lament the robbery or rape for a long time, but at that moment, you did the right thing. You made the right choice between the two options you were given.

An unhappy marriage is the same. You weighed whether or not to marry, and, at the moment of choice, you chose to marry. No one else made that choice for you. That's how the best judgments we make at each moment accumulate to create our present situation.

Let's say you are sentenced to 10 years in prison for assault because you lost your temper and beat someone up. Later, you might regret that choice, but at the moment you assaulted the other person, you told yourself they deserved it even if you knew it could mean getting a long prison sentence. If someone had tried to stop you by reminding you that a Buddhist shouldn't act that way, you would have answered that you are not a Buddha. At that moment, you chose to act on your anger and go to prison rather than act like the Buddha. If you had to suppress your anger to become a Buddha, you would elect not to become one.

Just like the phrase, "You reap what you sow," all of us

arrived at our current state by the choices we continuously made along the way. Whether the result is good or bad, it's our own making. At the moment we act, we think we are doing the right thing, but later we come to regret it. At each instant along the way, we are convinced we're doing the right thing. But when we look back at our actions, it seems like we have done so many wrong things.

Why is that? Because we're foolish. Because we live with our eyes closed and don't see the world as it is. No one wants their life to go wrong. In our own way, we try to do the right thing at each moment. We bring suffering to ourselves because we are blinded to what will come as a result of our decisions. When a rat eats rat poison or a fish bites a lure, it thinks it's making the right choice because it didn't know any better. Ignorance is the cause of suffering. When you open your eyes and eliminate your ignorance, you will no longer suffer. To be free and happy, you should be awake at each moment, so the ignorance that causes such suffering doesn't arise.

If you do something foolish at some point, you have to willingly accept the consequences of your action. This is called the Law of Causality. However, people don't want to accept the consequences. After eating the rat poison, we writhe in agony, blaming the heavens or a previous life, and bewail our fate. We have to be responsible for our appearance, personality, and life. A married person has to be responsible for their marriage, parents should be responsible for the child they gave birth to, and, if employed, they have to be responsible as employees.

If you don't want to accept these responsibilities, you need to change your situation. It's not a problem if a single man dates one woman today and another tomorrow. However, if a married man has coffee with a woman other than his wife, this becomes a problem. It's a problem if his wife thinks it's a problem even if no one else does. However, men often think it's unfair for their wives to view it that way. They insist there is nothing wrong with simply having a cup of coffee with another woman. They get angry when their wives insist it's a problem. If they didn't want it to be a problem, they should have remained single.

We should all be able to look within ourselves. This is true not just for Buddhists. It's not about religion but about how we are going to live as human beings.

Choice and Responsibility

There was a stay-at-home wife whose husband graduated from a prestigious college, had a good job, earned a decent living, and came straight home from work every night. He was a morally flawless man, but his wife said she couldn't stand living with him. When I asked why, she told me that, since her childhood, her dream was having a husband with whom she could enjoy a cup of coffee at a café on weekends. It turns out her husband didn't share her sentiments. Her complaint wasn't that her husband was having affairs or being violent but that he was insipid. In her eyes, he was dull and boring. She wondered if he found any meaning in life when all he did was work, eat, and sleep. She wanted to realize her dream even if it led to a lower standard of living. Eventually, she found someone else. Once she'd achieved her goal of finding a man with whom she could have coffee, listen to music, and converse, she divorced her husband. Everyone, including her family and friends, told her she was crazy. They criticized her for leaving such a good husband, saying she had stupidly killed the goose that laid the golden egg. However, her dissatisfaction with her husband left her feeling that she had no other choice.

A long time ago, I also believed my thoughts were noble and others' were trivial. But through experience, I came to realize that the way that woman preferred romance over a stable marriage, and the way I liked to learn the Buddha's teachings even if it meant I would go to hell for it, were similar. She might think I was crazy living my life the way I did. In fact, many people have said to me, "Sunim, I have heard it is very dangerous in India. You could be shot to death. And the weather is so hot there that the temperature actually reaches plus 40° Celsius (or approximately 104° Fahrenheit). Why do you go out of your way to build schools in such a place when you don't even seem to be welcome there?"

People tell me they understand why I give Dharma talks in Korea as everyone there loves to hear them. But they can't understand why I go to India. There is no difference between saying, "What's the problem? How can you have a complaint about someone like your husband?" and saying, "What complaint could you have about the temple that would make you leave everything and go to India to build a school there?"

The number of people who support your decision is not the criteria for wanting to do something. To that woman and to me, what each of us wishes to do is equally important. We need to value each and every person. When I say we have to value others, it means we have to value our own dreams and ideals as well.

"When I value my dreams and ideals, I don't want to trample on the dreams and ideals of others. As I don't want my dreams and ideals to be destroyed by anyone else, I don't want to destroy the dreams and ideals of anyone else." That is the way we should think. In order to do this, we need to communicate with others. We need to listen to other people's dreams and ideals and value them as we value our own.

A Taste of Enlightenment

The problem is that we live our lives so irresponsibly. We like the color of one flower, the shape of another, and the leaf of a different flower. This is greed. When a man and a woman meet, they have different expectations. They want a romantic partner when dating, a good spouse when married, and a competent person when working.

Why do you think the woman with the romantic dream of being able to enjoy a cup of coffee with her husband every weekend divorced him? It was because she only valued her own dream and ideal but not that of her husband. She demanded her dream be fulfilled with no thought or care about the things her husband did for her. Her husband had probably asked himself what hadn't he done for her. But he hadn't tried to understand why his wife was so dissatisfied.

We need to look at ourselves first. If you are blinded by greed, you'll bring suffering to yourself. First, you need to get rid of your greed, and then choose what to value. Only at that point will your loving wife, husband, parent, or child not become an obstacle in your way. There are situations where, if you follow the wishes of your spouse, you can't volunteer for Jungto Society, and if you volunteer for Jungto Society, your spouse becomes an obstacle. In another case, if you listen to your parents, you can't volunteer for the Jungto Society, and if you still decide to volunteer for the organization, you will become an undutiful child. Being torn between the two choices and suffering from inner conflict are all due to the greed inside you.

It's easy to solve the problem if you reflect on yourself. However, it will be very difficult to find a solution if you blame others for the problem. What could be more unfortunate than the Jungto Society becoming an obstacle to your love, the wife you chose keeping you from realizing your ideal, the parents who gave birth to you and raised you becoming an obstacle in the path you want to follow, or the child who you gave birth to becoming a barrier to realizing your dream? These situations occur when we're not awake to ourselves.

The Principle of Acceptance

Our thoughts, opinions, and will are formed by the experiences and environment we grew up in, just as we speak Korean, Chinese, English, or French depending on what language we were exposed to when we were growing up. Depending on the food we ate as a child, we end up liking kimchi, mashed potatoes, fajitas, or pad thai.

This is the same as coloring on a white piece of paper. We can't say which color is good and which is bad. In nature, there are many species of flowers, all with different colors and shapes. Just like there are countless types of flowers, human beings have created a wide variety of cultures in this world. Maybe this diversity is a principle of nature.

However, when we look at the way we live, it seems like we're trying to preserve only a few species while destroying all the others. Just as we try to conserve certain plants and eliminate others, we place one culture, one religion, and one language at the center of our world and then consider other cultures, religions, and languages defective and inferior. Just as many biological species are disappearing, thousands of human cultures, languages, religions, and ethnic groups that have developed over hundreds of thousands of years are rapidly disappearing. It's important for the human race to protect not only biological species but also ethnic minorities, religions, and cultures. It is only fair to say that the level of our cultural maturity is still low. We are only now beginning to realize the need to protect the diversity of biological species but not the diversity of human cultures.

Taking it a step further, each of us needs to value other people's thoughts, habits, and feelings, but the truth is we don't. We don't even respect the thoughts and tastes of the people closest to us, much less anyone else's. We become angry and annoyed with or even hate and resent others because we put our thoughts, habits, and ideologies at the

A Taste of Enlightenment

center of our lives, and we don't tolerate anyone else's. When we say we're suffering, it means that we're sure we're right. We insist on our own thoughts, habits, and notions. If we let all of that go, we'd be left with nothing to be angry or annoyed about and no one left to hate.

This doesn't mean that we can't live the way we wish, since every individual may live according to their own preferences and inclinations. In nature, there are tens of thousands of plant species, but you have the freedom to plant the flowers you like best in your garden. Likewise, you can live your life according to your beliefs. For example, you can choose to live only with people who think like you. I'm simply saying that hating someone for thinking differently from you is wrong. Liking a person's face but not the way they think is the same as liking a flower's color but not its shape. Each flower has its own particular shape and color. You have to accept it as a whole. However, if you don't like it, you don't have to plant it. Suffering arises when you insist on only accepting the aspect you like about something and rejecting the aspect you don't like, when in truth, the two cannot be separated.

Therefore, when we are with others, we have to accept them

as they are. We are free to choose which flower to plant, but it's unrealistic and impossible to think we can choose just its color or its shape. If you choose someone because you liked something about that person, you also have to accept any aspects you don't like.

Let's take Jungto Society as an example. Members of the Jungto Society don't care much about a person's appearance, gender, or academic background. Of the many aspects that make a human being, we value their dreams and their aims the most. If one agrees with that prerequisite, that person can join us. Anything other than that is a private matter. Whether that person is a woman or a man and whatever habits they have are of little consequence.

So, we've established several rules. Jungto Society considers environmental matters to be important. An individual can choose to use toilet paper or water after going to the bathroom, but we agreed to live without toilet paper because it makes up the largest portion of household waste. To join Jungto Society, you need to agree with this aim and idea, but would you be considered a bad person if you didn't agree with this aim? Not at all. However, if you choose to become a member of the Jungto Society, you can't say that you have to use toilet paper because it's an individual preference. At the same time, Jungto Society shouldn't try to standardize the preferences and characteristics of all members, which is an impossible task anyway. Therefore, when you want to create an organization, you have to clearly define its characteristics, so people can decide whether they want to join.

In the same way, a number of choices are involved in the decision to get married. If you want to do everything your way, it's better for you to live alone. If you insist on doing things your way, and, at the same time, you want to enjoy married life, there will be conflicts. If you want to do whatever you want and only work with others to achieve a goal, but, like me, you don't want to be bothered with personal matters, you should live alone. If you want to get married, you can't live as you please. You have to adjust to your partner's needs. If you marry a woman whose dream is to listen to music over a cup of coffee with her husband at a café, you need to satisfy that need on a regular basis. If you don't, she'll complain. Her wish is not a fault. When you choose to marry a woman with such a wish, you need to take time to make that a part of your life. If you don't want to take the time, you shouldn't marry her. Husbands often hear their wives accuse them of acting as if their work is more important than their wives. So, you have to choose. You have to choose what is really more important.

It seems absurd, but that's how human psychology works. All human beings want someone they value to value them in return. For some people, having a cup of coffee is important but not who they have coffee with. For other people, the person who they have coffee with, not the coffee itself, is important. That's just one of the characteristics that a particular person has. Simply accept that for what it is. It's easy for us to judge such a person in certain ways, but that's only our opinion.

The Path to Loving Yourself
as Well as Others

People like to say that the world is complicated. But the world is just what it is, neither complicated nor uncomplicated.

The weather is the same. People make a fuss and turn on the air conditioner when it gets a little hot, and they turn on a heater when it gets a little cold. However, it's the people who are capricious; the weather has always been like that. Life would be impossible if the weather were always clear or always rainy. We're able to survive because it's sometimes sunny and sometimes rainy. People complain about the weather being sunny or rainy because it isn't the weather they want. We try to fit the world into a conceptual framework. If the world fits into our framework, we feel we understand it. But if it doesn't, we bemoan how complicated and confusing the world is. It never occurs to us that we might be viewing the world in the wrong way. It's just like trying to adjust your body to fit the clothes rather than adjusting the clothes to fit your body. Our thoughts are complicated, and our mind is ignorant. The world is neither complicated nor ignorant. The world is just what it is.

Still, we continue to insist on ourselves, our belongings, and our opinions. We keep bringing suffering to ourselves. Anger, irritation, sadness, maliciousness, and loneliness can be expressed with one word — suffering. Who makes us suffer like this? We do. In other words, if you're suffering, you are not respecting or valuing yourself. How would you view someone who drinks too much liquor, becomes an alcoholic, and suffers from physical pain? You would no doubt think they lost their health due to ignorance.

Likewise, our mind is pure in its essence, but we hate and blame others and torment ourselves when we get caught up in our thoughts. If you abuse yourself like this, who will value and love you? How can you value and love others when you don't love and value yourself? How can you know others when you don't know yourself? How can you liberate others when you can't liberate yourself? And how can you make others happy when you can't make yourself happy? It doesn't make any sense.

So, you need to value and love yourself first. Loving yourself means no longer abusing yourself or treating yourself badly. Valuing and loving yourself is the starting point for both loving others and being loved by them. You abuse yourself when you insist on having your way, insist that something is yours, and insist on your opinion.

We need to be vigilant all the time. We shouldn't get caught up in ourselves by constantly examining "Who am I?" We need to know that everything in the world is not ultimately ours. We need to know that even the tiniest grain of soil contains the grace of the entire universe and the efforts of all the people in it. Only then will we be able to truly value it and allow it to be used by someone who needs it.

Medicine is medicine when a sick person takes it, but it becomes poison when a healthy person does. Similarly, food is food when a hungry person eats it but is no longer food when it is eaten by someone who is full. Currently, we harm ourselves by eating unhealthy food due to our attachment to taste or by eating more than we need. This is a very foolish thing to do. We think it's a good thing because we've been doing it for a long time. We overeat, take medicine to help us digest it, and then grumble that we have to lose weight. We can understand a person going to the hospital because they haven't had enough to eat and they're malnourished. How can we make sense of people who constantly overeat and then check into the hospital for stomach aches, liposuctions, or gastric bypasses?

These things happen because we are not awake. They happen because we don't know ourselves and the nature of existence. In other words, they happen because we do not know the true reality of all things.

We complain all the time. Husbands are frustrated by their wives, wives by their husbands, and parents by their children. We are frustrated by our bosses, colleagues, and monks. We feel frustrated when people cut into lines at subway stations and bus stops. We feel that the world is a total mess.

We have a lot of things to complain about. However, are the things we complain about only happening now or only just this year? The truth is that the world was like this last year and the year before that, and the world will be like that next year and the year after that. It's like a game of Whack-a-Mole, where you hit one mole only to have another pop up. The faster you hit them, the faster the new ones pop up. You keep thinking that if your present wishes are fulfilled, you won't have any new wishes. This is not true. You feel your life would be better if you got another job, got married, had a child, or your child went to college. However, your worries and complaints only increase with time. Instead of your life becoming simpler, your worries increase. When you retire, do you think you will lead a more leisurely lifestyle? No, it will never be more leisurely.

Life gets busier and more complicated as you get older. Instead of becoming more leisurely, you face more and more obstacles. If you want to change the world in order to make your life easier, it won't happen until you die. This is true not just for this world but for the next world as well. This is the way the world is.

In reality, the world isn't complicated at all. It feels complicated because we don't understand how it works. For example, if an ordinary person looks under the hood of a car, they may be disheartened by the complexity of the arrangements of the car parts. But to a car mechanic, the structure doesn't look complicated at all. The world is the same. Things that have reasons to exist, exist at the places where they need to exist, and things that have reasons to happen, happen when they should.

Therefore, we need to relax, despite being in the midst of endless work but not because we have nothing to do. We should be free, despite being in the midst of all sorts of relationships, but not because we have severed all relationships. We need to be free amid all kinds of complications, just like the lotus that grows out of the mud but is not stained by it. Lotus leaves do not get stained because they have smooth surfaces. If we're not hindered by anything, nothing in this murky world can hinder us. That's why it is imperative that we continue to practice diligently.

How to Live
Happily and Freely

A student wrote me a long letter saying he had a question for me, so I asked him to come to see me in person. "What do you want to ask me?"

"Sunim, why do you do volunteer work?"

"If your mother ran a store but got sick and asked you to tend the store for her on the weekend, but you already had a plan to go on a date with your girlfriend, would you want to tend the store?"

"I wouldn't want to."

"Then, if I ask you to choose between tending your mother's store and going on a date with your girlfriend, which would you choose?"

"Going on a date with my girlfriend."

"In this case, would you feel bothered if your mother asked you to tend the store?"

"Yes, I would."

"Let's say you went on a date with your girlfriend, but a month later your mother died. At that point, which do you think would have been the better choice, going on a date with your girlfriend or helping your mother?"

"Of course, helping my mother would have been better."

"What will you think is better for your life when you look back a month, a year, ten years, twenty years from now? Helping your mother would have been better not only for your mother but also for you. Volunteer work is the same."

Doing volunteer work is helpful to others, but it's even more beneficial to the volunteer. Between helping a child who has fallen down to get up and tripping a child to make them fall down, which would be more beneficial to you? Putting aside the child's viewpoint, helping the child to get up is more beneficial to you. Helping the child will make you feel proud, and that feeling will only grow over time. It's also beneficial to the child, so helping the child is a good choice. That's why we donate what we can, do volunteer work, and practice. Helping others is good for you. Practice works the same way. Practice is good for you. Living sensibly is good for you.

But we avert our gaze from things that are good for us. Sweet-tasting food might please our palate, but it could be bad for our health. However, if we're attached to the taste of food, we eat food that tastes good and end up hurting our health. Then, we end up regretting it. Liquor may taste good while we're drinking it, and it may make us feel good, but we'll be miserable the next day. There is no need to discuss the afterlife or the next life when we can easily perceive the next life just by examining our current day-to-day life. Repeating the same foolish behavior day after day is the principle behind reincarnation. We wander and suffer through countless lives within the cycle of birth and death.

We need to get away from this play built on illusion. I'm not telling you to explore abstract concepts, such as the existence of heaven or paradise after death. We have insisted on "I" countless times, but when we are asked who we are, we can't answer. We have claimed something is "mine" countless times, but we can't answer the question of why it is ours.

We are unable to see things as they are. Instead, we perceive them incorrectly because we're caught up in ideologies, theories, customs, habits, thoughts, and ideas. This is the same as taking the wrong path up a mountain from the start. Life is tiring because our thoughts are erroneous. That's why we can't solve life's problems until we die, no matter how hard we try. We cling to others for help. We cling to our husband, child, or the world, and, when that doesn't work, we cling to God or the Buddha. But praying to God or the Buddha won't solve our problems.

However, the problems in our lives end the moment we change our perspective. There will be no need to pray or ask for help in the first place. After changing our perspective, whatever we decide to do becomes easy. There will be nothing left to do but help others. I don't mean that you have to help them, but that everything you do and say will end up being helpful to others. Those who have a lot of work to do need the help of other people, but those who have nothing much to do have the time to help others.

Let's use food, clothing, and shelter as an example. When we try to secure good food, fancy clothing, and nice housing, things get complicated, and we struggle with the problems until our hair turns gray. However, the Buddha gave practitioners a simple solution to this problem. The Buddha told them to eat whatever is given, wear the clothing others throw away, and sleep under a tree or in a cave. The result was that, for the rest of their lives, those practitioners were able to help others with the time they would have wasted on securing food, clothing, and shelter.

As for clothing, a practitioner has one outfit that serves as their sleepwear, everyday clothes, and a Buddhist robe. As a result, practitioners don't have to waste any time figuring out what they should wear. How much clothing do you have? You had to spend time earning the money to buy all those outfits. And you have to spend time shopping for clothes and picking them out. Then, you have to spend time each morning trying to choose what to wear. The same goes for putting on make-up, eating, and sleeping. You work yourself to death to make money and spend it all on buying a house and furniture. You spend your time drinking, smoking, chit chatting, playing golf, etc. As for me, I don't spend any time drinking or chit chatting. People ask how I find the time to do so much work. Obviously, there's a great difference in the amount of work that can be done by those who spend most of their time eating, shopping, and playing, as opposed to a person like me who spends most of his time helping others.

If you tell a smoker to stop smoking, they won't understand it. However, would the Buddha, out of spite, tell you to stop doing something you like? No matter how expensive and high-quality a cigarette is, not smoking is better for your health. Some people boast that they spend hundreds of dollars on liquor, but not drinking alcohol is better for your health. People spend time making the money to buy cigarettes or alcohol, spend time harming their health by consuming cigarettes or drinks, and then have to spend time trying to recover their health. When you live like that, you don't have enough time for yourself, so you constantly cry out for help to the Buddha or God. We sentient beings live life in such a complicated and arduous way.

We are solely responsible for the present conditions of our lives. Did we intentionally live life the wrong way? No. We were just ignorant. We need to humbly accept the results of our choices and take responsibility for the things that have already happened, then change things so that, from now on, they are beneficial to us. We need to live a life that is good, whether we're alone or with someone else.

If you gain wisdom that enables you to live with a stubborn and problematic husband, you'll be able to live with anyone. Furthermore, you will be able to advise others on their problems, too. Since you have experienced all kinds of problems living with a difficult person, you'll know what to do when you listen to someone with a similar problem.

Maybe the Chinese philosopher and sage, Confucius, became wise because he had a difficult wife. However, to be fair, from the woman's position, you can't help but become a difficult wife if you live with a man like Confucius. So, we shouldn't absolutize Confucius's greatness. While in other people's eyes he appeared to be a great man, in his wife's eyes he had a lot of problems. From the wife's perspective, the husband is the problem, but from the husband's perspective, the wife is the problem. But if you look at things from a different perspective, the wife or husband may be like Confucius or the Buddha. We need to look at things in a new way. That is awakening. You don't have to drink from a skull or be tortured to be awakened. Every day, we encounter many opportunities to be awakened. If you accept the life given to you as it is, awakening is not far away.

If you want to experience awakening in everyday life, I recommend you attend an Awakening Retreat. Some say they don't need to because they are already awakened, and some say they just don't have time to attend because they're too busy. Don't procrastinate. Once you've actually experienced it, you'll know how helpful it is to your life. After experiencing the program, try to be awake and maintain awareness at every moment and practice diligently instead of stopping once the retreat is over.

Because of the habits you've acquired throughout your life, your behavior may not change quickly. It is very difficult to quit smoking at first, but once you quit, you'll feel good for a while. Later, when you face a stressful situation, you're likely to start smoking again. When things don't go well, we tend to go back to our old habits. That's why habits are scary. You have to overcome your habits rather than succumb to them.

To overcome a habit, you have to practice every day. If you practice steadily, you can control the temptation to return to the old habit. There is a big difference between a person who practices every day and a person who doesn't. You barely see any difference after practicing for a few days, but if you continue to practice, you'll be able to hold your ground when you face a difficult situation. In general, people get angry, annoyed, and consider themselves right, but if they continue to practice in the morning, they will naturally come to repent their actions. Sometimes, you might question why you continue to practice when you still get angry and annoyed. If you continue your practice, you'll have opportunities to repent, reminding yourself that you shouldn't act in such a way because you are a practitioner. Over time, the difference between a person who practices and one who doesn't widens significantly.

There are no special places to practice. The place you live is where you practice, and all discriminating thoughts that arise at each moment are the objects of your practice. If you live like that, you'll be at peace no matter what happens. You'll come to know that there are inevitable reasons behind your hair turning gray, getting wrinkles, becoming sick, going bankrupt, or someone dying. You realize these events aren't necessarily bad and could turn out to be good. You'll gain the wisdom to prevent bad things from happening by letting good things happen in their place. You will learn to humbly accept the consequences of your actions, and to avoid sowing the same seeds in the future, if you do not wish to suffer the same consequences.

Once while visiting Germany, I met a student who was studying hard to get his Ph.D. This student frequently attended my Dharma talks. To put it nicely, he had a deep Buddhist faith; to put it bluntly, he didn't study. I asked him whether he preferred listening to Dharma talks or studying for his Ph.D. He answered that he preferred listening to Dharma talks. So, I brought him to Korea. From his parents' perspective, this decision made their blood boil. Still, it was better for him. The reason he was getting a Ph.D. was to become happy and ultimately free, wasn't it? There was no need to put off such happiness for 10 to 30 years when he could live happily right now. The same is true for you.

You have to think deeply about your life. You have to examine whether you think you are right. It would be nice if you could do that by yourself but if you can't, you can get help from others to see yourself objectively. Once you do that, about 90% of your problems can be easily solved.

After that, you have to practice every day, reduce the time spent on unessential things, and focus on cultivating the mind. Awakening is not far away. It's right in front of us, and we can benefit from it at any time. It's not about pursuing some illusion that can never be attained or pursuing life after death. It's about how to live happily and freely beyond religion and religious sects. Awakening is making the effort to achieve such happiness and freedom in our present lives.

Life is full of uncertainty. Enlightenment or nirvana means living without making anything into a problem, no matter what happens. When it rains, rain is a good thing. When it's clear, clear skies and sunny weather are good things. When it's cold, being cold is a good thing, and, when it's hot, being hot is a good thing. I hope you live such a free and happy life.

Ven. Pomnyun Sunim

Ven. Pomnyun Sunim is a peace activist who delivers messages of peace and reconciliation, a humanitarian activist who provides various forms of aid to developing countries, a thinker who is paving the way toward a new alternative civilization, and an awakened practitioner. In 1988, he founded the Jungto Society, a community of practitioners who vowed to free themselves from suffering and devote themselves to serving others and the world by leading the life of a bodhisattva.

Ven. Pomnyun Sunim's Dharma talks are clear and straightforward. He has an exceptional ability to explain the Buddha's teachings in simple, contemporary language. As a result, his spoken and written messages go straight to the heart of the matter and enable people to redirect their eyes inward and self-reflect. Furthermore, the esoteric content of Buddhist sutras come to life through his wisdom, intuition, and insight.

As of April 2022, YouTube videos of Sumin's Dharma talks have had more than 1.7 billion views. He shares his wisdom with the general public on how to free themselves from suffering and how to become happy through his Dharma Q&As and the Happiness School program. To date, he has delivered more than 12,000 Dharma Q&As in South Korea and about 300 Dharma Q&As in other countries around the world, including the 115 talks he gave during his global tour in 2014. Also, since the Covid-19 pandemic began in 2020, Ven. Pomnyun Sunim has been interacting with hundreds of thousands of people through his weekly online Dharma Q&As in Korean, and bi-weekly talks in English. (See his website: https://pomnyun.com/)

Among the more than 50 books Ven. Pomnyun Sunim has published in Korean so far, the most notable are *Things Are Good as They Are Now, Buddha,* and *Commentary on the Diamond Sutra.* His books encompass

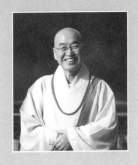

a wide range of subjects. His books, *Words of Wisdom for Newlyweds*, *Becoming Happier*, and *I Am a Decent Person*, provide insightful advice to young people. *Lessons for Life* is a guidebook for people living in modern society. *Prayer: Letting Go* is a manual for lay practitioners. *Practice Guidebook for Teachers* imparts wisdom for teachers. *The River of Life Flows* discusses an alternative solution to the environmental problem. And *Why Is Unification Necessary?* offers a vision for peace and unification on the Korean peninsula.

Some of these books have been translated into other languages, such as English, French, Thai, Japanese, Chinese, and Vietnamese. Eight books have been translated into English, including *Awakening*, *True Freedom*, *Prayer*, and *Monk's Reply to Everyday Problems* to list a few. Six books have been translated into Chinese, 3 books into Thai, 2 books into Japanese, 2 books into Vietnamese, and 1 book into French. Among the few books that were translated into multiple languages is *My Happy Way to Work*, which was translated into Thai, Chinese, Japanese, and Vietnamese. Another is *Becoming Happier*, which has English, Vietnamese, and Japanese versions.

Based on the idea that practice at the individual level goes hand in hand with social engagement, Ven. Pomnyun Sunim has engaged in extensive peace initiatives for various causes including a peaceful unification of the Korean Peninsula, refugee support, international relief efforts, and interfaith reconciliation and cooperation. Throughout the years, he has received numerous awards in recognition for his efforts. In 2002, he received the Ramon Magsaysay Award for Peace and International Understanding, and he was presented the 37th Niwano Peace Prize in 2021.